W9-DJH-327

"What if Jeremy makes an offer?" Elizabeth asked.

"I guess I'll have to deal with it if it happens—but it probably won't. A commitment-phobe like Jeremy isn't likely to actually buy a bridal shop."

Elizabeth nodded. "Yeah, you're right. I'll never forget. . ."

When she didn't finish her sentence, Cindi offered a half smile. "You can say it. He jilted me right before high school graduation. I won't forget it, either, but I got over it a long time ago." At least she thought she had—until now. "I went away to college, and he went into the army. Besides, I don't think he was a Christian, so it wouldn't have worked out between us anyway."

"It's just weird how it all happened. One day he seemed to be so into you, and the day after you told him about your scholarship and acceptance to the University of Georgia, he suddenly acted so cold."

"Yeah, that was weird, but at least it showed me that side of him. Good thing I found out early, huh?"

"I guess." Elizabeth shrugged. "It was so sudden, though. I kept thinking there was more to it than that."

"Maybe," Cindi said. "But I remember what the pastor said when he caught me in the hallway crying. He reminded me that not only did Jeremy not seem to be a believer, but he heard Jeremy had a history of breaking girls' hearts and I needed to count my blessings."

DEBBY MAYNE has been a freelance writer all her adult life, starting with slice-of-life stories in small newspapers and then moving on to parenting articles for regional publications and fiction stories for women and girls. She has been involved in all aspects of publishing, from the creative side to editing a national health magazine to freelance proofreading for several book publishers. Her belief that all blessings come from the Lord has given her great comfort during trying times and gratitude for when she is rewarded for her efforts. She lives on the west coast of Florida with her husband and two daughters.

Books by Debby Mayne

HEARTSONG PRESENTS
HP625—Love's Image
HP761—Double Blessing

Don't miss out on any of our super romances. Write to us at the following address for information on our newest releases and club information.

Heartsong Presents Readers' Service
PO Box 721
Uhrichsville, OH 44683

Or visit www.heartsongpresents.com

If the
Dress Fits

Debby Mayne

Heartsong Presents

This book is dedicated to Kim Llewellyn, Tara Spicer, and Kathy Carmichael—friends who have stuck with me through everything.

I'm also thankful to my fabulous agent, Tamela Hancock Murray, for her energy and enthusiasm.

A note from the Author:
I love to hear from my readers! You may correspond with me by writing:

Debby Mayne
Author Relations
PO Box 721
Uhrichsville, OH 44683

ISBN 978-1-59789-900-0

IF THE DRESS FITS

Copyright © 2008 by Debby Mayne. All rights reserved. Except for use in any review, the reproduction or utilization of this work in whole or in part in any form by any electronic, mechanical, or other means, now known or hereafter invented, is forbidden without the permission of Heartsong Presents, an imprint of Barbour Publishing, Inc., PO Box 721, Uhrichsville, Ohio 44683.

All of the characters and events in this book are fictitious. Any resemblance to actual persons, living or dead, or to actual events is purely coincidental.

Our mission is to publish and distribute inspirational products offering exceptional value and biblical encouragement to the masses.

PRINTED IN THE U.S.A.

one

Tears stung the back of Cindi Clark's eyes as she reached out and gently stroked the satin bodice of the bridal gown she'd lovingly put on the mannequin. She'd dreamed of working in a bridal shop for as long as she could remember, and here she was, the owner, and less than a year before she turned thirty.

She should be happy, but her parents had announced they were splitting up. If they couldn't stay together, how could she, in good conscience, keep perpetuating the myth of happily-ever-after? With a heavy heart, she'd contacted a commercial Realtor from her old neighborhood to list the shop, and now her place was for sale.

"Sometimes I wish I could buy the place," Elizabeth said.

Cindi turned around to face her longtime best friend and only full-time employee. "Yeah, me, too."

"But without you here, it wouldn't make sense. Besides, I really want kids."

Cindi chuckled. "I used to want them, too."

Elizabeth dropped the tiara back into the box she'd been unpacking, crossed the showroom, and gently placed her hand on Cindi's arm. "I know your parents' split is hard on you, but you shouldn't become jaded over it."

With a nod, Cindi forced a smile. "Yeah, I know. I just don't want to participate in something that's probably going to end in heartache eventually. I mean, look at the number of brides who come in a year later and say it didn't work." She turned back to the gown and sighed. "Too bad marriage goes downhill right after the wedding."

5

"That's not always true, ya know." Elizabeth stared at the dress Cindi was putting on the mannequin. "I think this is my favorite dress in the shop."

"They're all your favorite," Cindi teased. "You're like I was a few years ago—filled with all kinds of romantic notions of a fairy-tale marriage to match the wedding."

Elizabeth shrugged as she turned and headed back to her unpacking. "Personally, I don't see anything wrong with that. So what if I'm a romantic at heart? I have a good marriage."

"You're unusual. That's not the reality for most people."

Before Elizabeth had a chance to argue, Cindi pulled her key ring out of her pocket, went to the door, and unlocked it. Cindi was relieved they had an early appointment for a fitting. She was growing weary of Elizabeth trying to talk her out of selling.

Her appointment showed up right on time with her mother right on her heels. Angelina Dillard was a soft-spoken girl, the polar opposite of her clearly excitable mother.

"Would you like some orange juice?" Cindi asked.

Angelina nodded, but her mother adamantly shook her head no. "Orange juice has calories, and I don't want my daughter bloated for the fitting."

Her daughter scowled.

"Maybe afterward, then." Cindi took a step back and gestured around the showroom. "Why don't the two of you peruse the racks and find some different styles to try? We can alter any of these dresses for a perfect fit."

Mrs. Dillard scanned the room then zeroed in on one of the front racks. "I want to see my daughter in this dress," Mrs. Dillard demanded. She turned to look over the rest of the assortment then pointed toward the circular rack by the back wall. "And that one over there."

Cindi turned to Angelina with a questioning gaze. "Is there

anything else you'd like to try?"

Angelina barely had her mouth open when her mother grabbed another dress off the rack. "Let's see how this one looks."

"Mom, I really don't like the full skirts," Angelina said softly. "I'd rather—"

Mrs. Dillard flipped her hand at the wrist. "How would you know what you like when you haven't even put one of these on? I think you'll look like a princess in a full skirt."

Cindi glanced at Elizabeth and winked before turning back to Angelina. "Why don't you try on several different styles before you decide?"

Elizabeth had already pulled a few off the rack and headed back to the fitting room. They'd seen this same scenario many times—the overbearing mother dragging the weary future bride through the store. And rather than pick sides, Cindi and Elizabeth managed to remain neutral as they tried to make peace during one of the most stressful times in the bride's life.

As Cindi listened to Angelina's desires and thoughts about the dresses, she directed Elizabeth to bring in more gowns, each one getting closer to what the bride wanted. They'd learned early that instantly jumping from one side to the other wasn't the best way to handle this touchy situation.

The skirts grew less full and more formfitting with each try-on, and the long sleeves gradually shrank to three-quarter sleeves, short sleeves, then sleeveless until Angelina finally had what she obviously wanted to begin with. As Cindi zipped the shiny white satin dress with the floral lace overlay on the bodice, both Angelina and her mother beamed.

"See?" Mrs. Dillard said. "I told you I'd find the perfect gown. This is absolutely lovely on you." She took a step back and studied her daughter in silence.

Cindi met Angelina's gaze then quickly glanced down to keep from smiling. Angelina turned back to face herself in the three-way mirror. "This is the one I want."

Her mother's reticence quickly evaporated. She sprang back into action, grabbing a hunk of material at the waist. "This dress is way too big for my daughter. It needs to be taken in here. . . ." She pointed to the hem. "And there. It's way too long. Is there any way you can hem it without ruining the train?"

Elizabeth popped into the room sporting a pincushion on her wrist. "Absolutely. We do it all the time."

"It has to be perfect," Mrs. Dillard screeched. "We've invited everyone from the country club, and they'll notice everything."

Cindi felt that awful, familiar constriction in her chest. "Angelina will be a beautiful bride." She nearly choked on the words, but she meant it.

Mrs. Dillard beamed. She reached out and smoothed her daughter's hair. "She sure will. By the time we get her hair done and all my heirloom diamonds on her, she'll make all my friends jealous."

Angelina looked annoyed. She'd obviously had this conversation with her mother before.

"Even now, with her hair down and no jewelry, she's beautiful," Elizabeth said.

Before Cindi had a chance to agree, Mrs. Dillard started flapping her jaw again, going on and on about the guest list, yapping about how all the girls would swoon and wish they were the bride—all the wrong reasons for this wedding. Cindi had heard it all before. The last bride who'd tied the knot cried at the first fitting and said she'd changed her mind about the wedding and wanted to elope. Elizabeth had managed to soothe her nerves.

"Would you like some orange juice now?" Cindi offered. "We also have some muffins if you're hungry."

Angelina smiled and nodded. "I'm starving."

Mrs. Dillard frowned. "Are they low-fat?"

"I believe we have some low-fat in the freezer," Elizabeth said. "I can thaw them in the microwave."

"Never mind," Mrs. Dillard said. "We don't have that kind of time."

Angelina frowned and stared at her shoes.

Cindi recognized the look of dejection. "It'll only take a minute." She turned to Elizabeth. "Why don't you pour the orange juice while I get a couple of muffins ready?"

They scurried to action, leaving no room for argument. Even from the back room, they could hear Mrs. Dillard talking about watching every single bite because Angelina needed to stay slim and trim—at least until after the wedding.

"Don't let it get to you," Elizabeth whispered as they arranged the tray of orange juice and muffins.

"We just need to make sure Angelina gets the gown she wants," Cindi agreed. "The rest of it is out of our hands." She squeezed her eyes shut and said a silent prayer for the patience to continue working with Mrs. Dillard.

When she opened her eyes again, Elizabeth had already carried the tray to the showroom where Angelina and her mother sat on the love seat in the corner. Cindi joined them and gave her talk about how they wouldn't have to worry about a thing related to the dress because Cindi's Bridal Boutique had the experience with all the details ironed out.

The phone rang, so Cindi excused herself, leaving Elizabeth to finish the first session with the Dillard women. It was her Realtor.

"I have a potential buyer for the shop," Fran Bailey said.

Cindi's heart thudded with an odd mix of anticipation and

unexpected sadness. "Good." That's all that would come out.

"He wants to see the shop tomorrow afternoon, if that's convenient."

Cindi opened her appointment book before she realized what Fran had said. "He? As in a man?"

"Yes, he's a very successful businessman who likes the thought of owning a bridal shop."

How odd. In all the scenarios Cindi had envisioned, a male buyer hadn't even crossed her mind. "Well, I guess that would be okay."

Fran chuckled. "I know his mother, and she's a very nice lady. Besides, we can't very well turn down potential male buyers."

"Oh, I understand. I'm booked until noon, but after that I'm free until two tomorrow afternoon."

"Excellent!" Fran said. "I'll bring him by at one. He's already seen the shop from the outside, and he wants to come in and take a look around inside."

"I'll stay out of the way," Cindi offered.

"Um, he asked that you stick around."

"I thought you said—"

Fran interrupted. "I know when you listed I said it's best for you to make yourself scarce in the beginning stages, but occasionally buyers make specific requests. I told him it might be better to wait until he's closer to a decision, but he insisted."

Cindi paused for a moment and tried to imagine why someone would insist she be there. "I'll do whatever you feel I should," she finally told Fran, "if you think that would help sell this place."

&

Jeremy took another spin around the block and slowed down as he got close to Cindi's Bridal Boutique. He was amazed at how much of herself she'd put into the window display. If someone had shown him pictures of a dozen bridal shops and said one of them was Cindi Clark's, he would have picked this one without a second's hesitation.

He came to a near stop and stared at the window, half hoping he'd see Cindi and half hoping he wouldn't. Ever since she went away to college, he'd wondered about her. The breakup had ripped him up inside, and he wished he'd handled things differently. He should have been completely up front with her rather than acting like the tough guy. But he was a kid back then. What did he know?

The car behind him honked, so after a quick glance in the rearview mirror, he accelerated. He needed to head back to his parents' condo in Roswell.

He pulled into the condo parking lot right after his mother, who'd just closed and locked her car door. She smiled as she turned to him. "Productive day?" she asked.

Jeremy shrugged as he loosened his tie. "I've narrowed down a few places to look at."

"It would be nice for you to find a business here in the Atlanta area so we can see more of you."

He gently put his arm around the woman who'd sacrificed so much for him and his brother. "I know. After I nail down a business, I'll look for a house."

"You can buy the condo at the other end of our building," she quickly offered.

With a chuckle, he shook his head. "As tempting as that is, I'm afraid I need to be a little farther away so you won't feel like you have to cook for me every night."

"I really don't mind," she argued.

"I know you don't, and that's very sweet." He leaned over and kissed her cheek. "But I'll be fine. Speaking of dinner, how about I take you and Dad out tomorrow after work?"

"Think we might have something to celebrate?" she asked as she slowed her pace.

"Maybe."

❧

Cindi had arrived early to make sure the showroom was perfect for the Realtor. "I totally don't get why I have to meet this guy."

"I'm sure he just wants to ask some questions about the profitability," Elizabeth said.

"Probably, but I'm thinking he'll take one look at the place and leave when he realizes we're strictly a bridal shop." She rolled her eyes. "After all, what would a man want a place like this for?"

"Maybe it's for his wife or something."

"I didn't think about that. Whatever the case, I want to make sure nothing's out of place."

Elizabeth tilted her head back and laughed. "Nothing's ever out of place here. You're the most meticulous person I know."

Cindi took a rag out from behind the counter, squirted some furniture polish on it, and took one more swipe at the wooden shelves by the desk. "That'll have to do." She went to the back and tossed the rag into the hamper to take home later.

When she came back out to the front, Elizabeth was standing at the front of the store chatting with Fran and her client, who looked amazingly like. . .

"Jeremy?" she squeaked.

The man glanced at Fran, who cast a curious look first at Cindi then at Jeremy. Then he took a tentative step toward her. Cindi felt numb from the tip of her toes to the top of her head—she couldn't budge, she was so shocked. She felt she'd just taken a giant step back in time—and her tall, dark, and handsome boyfriend had just entered the room. His brow-hooded brown eyes had a few crinkles around them, but she would have recognized him anywhere.

After a couple of seconds, she cleared her throat and looked at Fran. "Is this your. . .client?"

Fran nodded. "I understand you two knew each other a long time ago."

"We were high school friends," Jeremy quickly said.

"Um, Jeremy," Elizabeth blurted, "it's nice to see you after all these years."

Jeremy offered a grin. "Nice to see you, too, Elizabeth. Things going well for you?"

Cindi turned to Elizabeth, who clamped her mouth shut and shrugged as she took a small step back. Elizabeth was obviously just as surprised as she was.

"So this is what you've been doing since college, huh?" Jeremy asked, breaking the short silence.

"Yes." The lump in Cindi's throat was so big she was afraid to try to say more.

"Nice," he replied with a nod as he walked around, looking everything over, making Cindi feel she was being scrutinized. "Very nice."

"Why are you here, Jeremy?" Cindi asked.

His attention quickly returned to her. "I like buying thriving homegrown businesses and taking them to the next level."

Fran's smile widened. "And he's been quite successful at it."

"So I've heard," Cindi said. "You don't live here, so how can you run a bridal shop?"

"I'll just hire someone to work it for me." He reached out and touched one of the gowns before pulling back to face her. "At least for a while. I'm thinking about moving back to Atlanta."

Cindi's shock had finally worn off, replaced by annoyance. "This isn't exactly the kind of business someone can hire unskilled workers to run."

Fran quickly dropped her smile. "Perhaps it wasn't such a good idea for the two of you to be here together so early in the process. Why don't we come back later, Jeremy?"

"No, that's okay. I'll just take a quick look around, and maybe Cindi can show me her books."

As tempted as she was to tell him her place was no longer for sale, Cindi just nodded. His appearance at her store had taken her completely by surprise—she was afraid she'd slip up and say or do the wrong thing.

She and Elizabeth stuck close together the rest of the time Jeremy was in the shop. A customer came in, so she didn't have a chance to show him her books. As soon as he and Fran left, Elizabeth turned to her, eyes wide, forehead crinkled, and slowly shook her head.

"I never saw that one coming. That totally surprised me."

Cindi snorted. "You and me both."

"What are you gonna do?"

"What can I do? Never in a million years would I have expected to see Jeremy Hayden thinking about buying my store."

"You can take it off the market."

"I know, but I don't think I'll do that."

"What if Jeremy makes an offer?" Elizabeth asked.

"I guess I'll have to deal with it if it happens—but it probably won't. A commitment-phobe like Jeremy isn't likely to actually buy a bridal shop."

Elizabeth nodded. "Yeah, you're right. I'll never forget. . ."

When she didn't finish her sentence, Cindi offered a half smile. "You can say it. He jilted me right before high school graduation. I won't forget it, either, but I got over it a long time ago." At least she thought she had—until now. "I went away to college, and he went into the army. Besides, I don't think he was a Christian, so it wouldn't have worked out between us anyway."

"It's just weird how it all happened. One day he seemed to be so into you, and the day after you told him about your scholarship and acceptance to the University of Georgia, he suddenly acted so cold."

"Yeah, that was weird, but at least it showed me that side of him. Good thing I found out early, huh?"

"I guess." Elizabeth shrugged. "It was so sudden, though. I kept thinking there was more to it than that."

"Maybe," Cindi said. "But I remember what the pastor said when he caught me in the hallway crying. He reminded me that not only did Jeremy not seem to be a believer, but he heard Jeremy had a history of breaking girls' hearts and I needed to count my blessings."

Their two o'clock appointment came in, so they spent the rest of their afternoon scurrying around, appeasing nervous brides and demanding mothers-of-the-brides. Cindi sometimes considered her job more of a counseling position than that of a bridal gown salesperson.

Elizabeth had to leave an hour early, so Cindi had the rest of the afternoon to herself. She had one more customer who wasn't due for a half hour, so she decided to rework the showroom window. She'd barely gotten the mannequin turned around when she saw the car slowing down in front of the shop. When she focused on the driver, she realized who it was. Jeremy. Her heart pounded hard and her mouth grew dry, but she forced herself to turn away.

❧

After all these times of driving by, he'd grown confident he wouldn't see Cindi—or more precisely that she wouldn't see him. But she had. He could tell when she recognized him because she jerked into quick action and moved out of direct view. She'd changed a little, but for the better. Her blond hair that once hung to her waist was now stylishly below her shoulders with long layers. Rather than contacts, she wore glasses that gave her more of an intellectual look yet didn't cover up her big blue eyes that sparked with emotion. He was happy to see she hadn't starved herself to get skinny like so many women her age did. She still had a pretty, round face and a smile that would light up any room.

He slammed his hand on the steering wheel. For the first time since becoming a businessman, he was unsure of himself. All his other business acquisitions had been effortless and calculated. This one, however, was nothing but an emotional roller-coaster ride. He'd heard the rumor that Cindi Clark owned a boutique of some sort. Then as soon as he spotted Cindi's Bridal Boutique in Fran's listing book, he remembered his old high school flame's dreams, and the name *CINDI* on the sign jumped out at him. Just by chance it was hers, he asked. Fran had given him a questioning look but nodded.

That was the last time he'd circle the block. It was time to leave her alone until he had more of a chance to think of what to do next. He looked at his watch and saw it was almost time for his dad to get home from work. He'd promised to take them out to dinner. He pulled out his cell phone and called his mom.

"We understand if you're too busy," she said.

Jeremy laughed. "I'm never too busy to take my favorite people out. I'll be there in half an hour. Think you can be ready then?"

"I'm ready, and I'm sure your father will be very quickly. All he'll want to do is change clothes and wash his hands."

"The timing will be good, then," Jeremy said.

"Where are you taking us?"

He laughed. "It's a surprise."

"You know we don't care where you take us. We're easy to please."

"Yes, I know, Mom, but I want to treat you and Dad to something wonderful."

"Just don't go getting any ideas of taking us someplace too fancy."

After he hung up, he paused and considered where he'd planned to take his parents. Atlanta Fish Market in Buckhead was one of the finest restaurants in the area, and he doubted his folks had ever been there. What if they didn't like it? Maybe it would make them uncomfortable.

Oh well. If he pulled into the parking lot and they insisted on going someplace else, he'd call from his cell phone and cancel their reservations. But he wanted to at least try to give them something they weren't likely to do for themselves. With money scarce during his childhood, his mother pinched pennies at the grocery store. They rarely went out for dinner. They sacrificed even more when they moved him and his brother to their first house right before he started high school. And they waited until both boys were gone before selling the house and buying the condo.

A few minutes after he arrived at their place, his dad came walking out of the bedroom all dressed up in his best navy suit and tie. "You don't think I'd want my son to outshine his old dad, do you?"

"I'll never outshine my dad," Jeremy said.

His mom squeezed between them and hooked her arms in theirs. "I'm the luckiest girl in the world to be with the two most handsome men in Atlanta."

Jeremy's dad wanted to drive, but Jeremy was more insistent. Since his own car was a two-seater, they took his dad's car. "You two sit in the backseat, and I'll play chauffer."

As soon as he pulled up to the Atlanta Fish Market, his

mother let out a sound he'd never heard her make, causing him to glance in the rearview mirror. "You okay back there?"

Her eyes round and wide, she nodded. "Can you afford this place?"

Jeremy's heart sank. He had a feeling she'd make him turn around and go someplace else—like Old Hickory House where the food was good but not nearly as pricey and much more down-home.

"Mom, I wouldn't take you here if I couldn't afford it." He paused before adding, "It is okay with you, isn't it?"

She nodded then broke into giggles. "Imagine me eating at a place like this. Son, you're so good to us."

❧

The next morning Cindi arrived at the shop early to look over her books. Fran had called late the previous day and said she was bringing Jeremy back. Cindi had mixed feelings. On the one hand, she didn't want to sell her business to an absentee owner, but on the other hand, she wanted to show him she was doing well.

Before opening her computer spreadsheet, she said a silent prayer for the ability to know what to do and the emotional stability to get through this. She'd been surprised to see Jeremy, but even more shocked at how she felt after all these years. The attraction was still there, but there was something else. The way he looked at her showed something she couldn't quite put her finger on. It was almost as though he was as nervous about seeing her as she was about seeing him.

She looked everything over and made sure all the fields were filled in. Between her and Elizabeth, the books had been painstakingly maintained. They were a good team. Too bad she'd lost faith in her business.

All the numbers balanced, and everything looked great. She closed the software program and walked around the shop once more to make sure it was sparkling. Even if she didn't sell it to Jeremy, she had pride in her work.

The phone rang. It was Elizabeth calling to let her know she'd been asking around about Jeremy and had learned that not only was he a successful businessman as they already knew, but he bought and sold businesses to turn a quick profit. "He's a business flipper."

"Thanks, Elizabeth," Cindi said, "but I already knew that." Jeremy had become somewhat of a celebrity among a bunch of the guys they graduated with because he'd made something of himself—at least in their eyes.

"Don't let him do that to something you've worked so hard for. I'd hate to watch all your blood, sweat, and tears go down the drain just because he sees a golden opportunity."

Cindi assured her she'd think before acting on this deal. After she got off the phone, she leaned against the counter and closed her eyes.

Her mind flashed back to the pain of Jeremy's breakup. It had taken years to get past the pain—until now.

The flash of sunlight on the door as it opened caught her attention. She spun around and saw Jeremy. Alone.

Fran was nowhere in sight.

two

"Fran's meeting me here," Jeremy said before Cindi had a chance to ask. "I was hoping you and I could talk first."

"There's really not much to talk about."

He stepped closer—so close, in fact, Cindi was certain he could hear her heartbeat. He stopped about three feet away. She slowly let out the breath she was holding.

"I'm impressed with what you've done," he said softly.

Her mind raced with all sorts of comebacks, but she didn't want to risk letting him know how hurt she'd been, so she didn't let any of them out. "I've worked hard for all of it."

"I can see that. Looks to me like you haven't missed a single detail. What I don't understand is why you'd get this far and want to sell."

She shrugged and turned away. "I don't know. Maybe I'm ready to move on."

"That's not like you, Cindi."

Suddenly she felt a burst of adrenaline mixed with anger. "No, it isn't, is it?" She spun around to face him. "I'm the steady type. The kind of girl who stays with things unless there's a very good reason to quit."

He tightened his jaw and looked down. She instantly regretted showing her frustration, but it was too late now.

"I'm probably going to make an offer," he said.

"Fine." Cindi saw Fran approaching the shop, so she turned to face the door.

"Oh, good," Fran said as she made her entrance. "You're here. I was afraid you'd sleep in after last night." She offered

Jeremy a conspiratorial wink.

Last night? And what was with that wink? Maybe he'd had a date he'd told Fran about. An annoying, unexpected pang of jealousy shot through Cindi. She looked away to prevent either of them from noticing.

"Thanks for recommending Atlanta Fish Market," he said.

A date to one of the best restaurants in the entire Atlanta area. Whoever she is must be special. Cindi bit her bottom lip.

"I was afraid my mom would balk," he continued. "She's always hated spending too much money."

"Yes, I know," Fran said with a smile. "She and I have gone bargain hunting together many times. Did your dad like the seafood?"

A double date with his parents. Sounds serious. Maybe he is buying this bridal shop for the woman in his life.

"He loved it. In fact, he said if he'd known how good it was, he would have taken Mom there before. I was surprised I was able to get reservations on such short notice."

Fran nodded. "It's not too hard to squeeze in a table for three at the last minute."

Table for three? So he went there with his parents and no date? To her dismay, a flood of relief nearly overcame her.

Jeremy turned to Cindi. "I've been staying with my parents while I look for real estate, and I wanted to do something nice for them."

"Dinner at the Atlanta Fish Market is *very* nice," she agreed.

"Maybe I can take you there next time?" he asked.

"Um. . .I don't think so."

A stricken look crossed his face. "Oh, I'm sorry. I didn't even ask if there was someone. . . I should have known."

Cindi started to say there was no one in her life, but she refrained. She hadn't dated anyone more than a couple of times since high school, but he didn't have to know he'd left her so raw that she didn't trust herself in a relationship.

"Speaking of parents," he said with a smile, "how are yours? I'll never forget those Friday nights with your family playing Monopoly and watching Nickelodeon."

"Um, my parents. . ." She didn't feel like discussing their split, so she figured she might as well just be general. "They're fine."

"Still doing the Friday night thing?"

Cindi slowly shook her head. "Not since Chad and I moved out."

He smiled and nodded. "Makes sense. I guess they must be doing their own thing these days. Well, good for them." He turned to Fran. "I was just about to ask Cindi if I can take a look at her records. Ready to get started?"

Cindi turned toward the tiny office in the back, then heard someone come in. She turned around in time to see a harried woman nearly dragging a younger woman who looked as though she'd rather be anywhere but there.

"I need a gown in a size six," the woman demanded. "Whaddya got in stock?"

"What time is your appointment?" Cindi asked.

The woman waved her hand as if she couldn't be bothered. "I don't have an appointment. No time for that. I caught my daughter in the nick of time—she was about to elope, but I caught her—and we need a gown real quick."

"We normally. . ." Cindi sucked in a breath while she decided what to do. This wasn't the first time someone needed a wedding gown on the spur of the moment, but she never had a potential buyer of the shop standing there waiting for her to finish her business before.

Jeremy nodded toward the customers, a smirk of amusement on his face. "Go ahead and take care of business. I'll wait."

Cindi licked her lips, smoothed her hands over her slacks, and tried to regain her composure. "We keep a few samples in stock. Do you have a particular style in mind?"

"Something decent," the middle-aged woman said as her daughter sulked by the door. "I don't want anything showing, if you know what I mean."

Cindi leaned over to get a handle on what the bride wanted. "Do you prefer a full gown or something more fitted?"

The younger woman just shrugged and turned completely around. Her mother, on the other hand, knew exactly what she wanted. "Long sleeves, full gown, lots of lace, long train, the whole nine yards."

"Mama," the girl said. "Please stop. Eric and I just want a quiet little wedding in a park."

"That's nonsense, Melissa. You're the only daughter I've got, and I'm not about to let you go off and get married by some justice of the peace in a filthy park somewhere."

Cindi's heart went out to the young woman, but she couldn't get involved. She stood there and waited before doing anything.

The older woman spun back around. "You heard me. I need to get the dress today."

"Our alterations person isn't in yet, but she can get right on it once she's here," Cindi explained.

"No time for that. We have to find something that fits off the rack."

To Cindi's surprise, Melissa finally gave in and tried on everything her mother picked out. However, she clearly felt miserable in all the dresses.

Exasperated, the mother left the fitting room saying they weren't leaving until they found the perfect dress. Once she was gone, Cindi turned to the bride.

"Did you have something in mind?" she asked.

Melissa sighed. "I really didn't want a traditional wedding dress. They're too fussy for me."

"Maybe I can help you out. We carry a collection that has simple lines." She paused and gave Melissa a chance to think.

"Since it doesn't look like I have any choice in this, I guess it wouldn't hurt to try one on."

Her mother breezed back into the fitting room with the most ornate dress in the shop slung over her arm. She shoved it at Melissa. "Here, try this."

Cindi offered the bride a sympathetic smile. "Why don't you work on getting into that while I go find a dress in our most exquisite line that's the latest rage with celebrity brides this year."

"Latest rage? Celebrity brides?" Melissa's mother asked. "What's that?"

"I'll bring one in for you to look at," Cindi replied. "In the meantime, since you went to the trouble of getting that one, why don't you help her into it?"

She gently closed the door behind her. "I'm really sorry, Fran, but Elizabeth isn't here yet and. . ."

"Don't worry about it. Jeremy said he doesn't mind waiting."

Cindi glanced around. "Where is he?"

"I sent him on an errand so you wouldn't feel so rushed. I'm enjoying just looking around at all the gorgeous gowns. Take your time."

Cindi relaxed a little since Jeremy wasn't in the show-room pacing. She went to the area where she kept samples that were for sale and pulled out one of the dresses with the cleanest lines. It was a brushed satin with a sweetheart neckline and three-quarter sleeves. It had a short train and a small amount of lace overlay on the bodice—just enough to make the mother happy.

When she opened the door to the fitting room, she saw the

anguished look on Melissa's face. She had to admit the dress totally overwhelmed the petite young woman.

"Now that's what I call a wedding dress," her mother said. "Isn't she the most gorgeous bride you've ever seen?"

"She is very pretty, but I'm not sure. . ." Cindi's voice trailed off as both Melissa and her mother watched her expectantly. She changed her mind midsentence, but she couldn't think of anything else to say.

"What's that?" her mother finally said after a few seconds of silence, pointing to the dress in Cindi's arms.

"Oh, it's one of the hottest dresses on the market. Celebrity brides are going crazy over this one."

Melissa's mother clasped her hands together as Cindi made a production of hanging it on the hook. She'd been in this business long enough to know a large part of selling a style was the unveiling.

Once she had it on the hook and arranged, she sucked in a breath, said a very short prayer, then turned around to see the reaction. At first there was none. Then a wide grin spread across the mother-of-the-bride's face.

"Yes, I've seen that one in the supermarket magazines. It's perfect."

Melissa's lips turned up into a grin. Cindi could tell she liked this one.

A few minutes later Melissa stood in front of the three-way mirror while her mother and Cindi admired her. "I like it," she finally said.

"We'll take it." Her mother turned her around and started unzipping the back.

"It won't take long to alter it so she can have a perfect fit," Cindi said. "When do you need it?"

"There's no time. The wedding's this afternoon in the small chapel behind the big church."

"This afternoon?" Cindi said, her voice cracking. She wasn't kidding, there wasn't any time.

"Yes, and it's a good thing I caught her heading out the door with her suitcase, or I never would've been able to witness my only daughter tying the knot. To think she didn't want me there or even bother to tell me..." Tears sprang to her eyes.

"Mama," Melissa said, "it's not that I didn't want you there. I just didn't want a big wedding with a lacy dress and a wedding cake taller than me."

"Well, consider yourself a fortunate girl that Kroger had a cancellation on a wedding cake and they were able to make the changes I wanted."

Cindi managed to get the dress ready and the two women out the door a half hour later. After they were gone, Fran turned to her and laughed.

"They're quite a pair, aren't they?"

"That's an understatement."

Fran shrugged. "There's something about a Southern mother-of-the-bride. It's not so much the bride's wedding as it is hers."

She'd pretty much summed it up. Jeremy had come back into the shop and was standing at the door until Melissa and her mother left. He joined Cindi and Fran.

"Very interesting," he said. "Does this sort of thing happen very often?"

"I can't say it's the first time," Cindi replied, "but it's not a regular occurrence."

He leaned back and laughed. "That's a relief."

Cindi lifted one eyebrow. "Situations like that have to be handled very carefully."

"Obviously," he said. "I guess that's something you can train whomever I get to manage the store to do."

"I guess." She pulled up the spreadsheet with all her sales

figures and inventory numbers, then printed them. "Here ya go. It's all there."

❧

Jeremy's hand brushed hers as she handed him the papers. He wanted more than that. He wanted to hold her hand, to pull her close, to take a deeper whiff of her floral scent. He wanted to brush her hair from her face and study the features he'd only seen in his mind for the past several years.

When he'd first decided to check out her business, he'd half hoped some of the chemistry between them would have faded, but it was there—stronger than ever. He wondered if she felt it, too. It didn't appear so, based on the way she turned her back on him every chance she could get—including now.

"Sure you don't mind if I take these?" he asked, hoping she'd turn around and look at him again.

She tossed her hair over her shoulder but didn't face him head-on. "I have nothing to hide. If you like what you see, we can talk about it. If not, then that's fine, too."

For someone who had her business up for sale, she sure didn't seem to want it sold that badly. Or perhaps it was a ploy to make him want it more. Whatever the case, she wasn't desperate. And he liked that.

"Anything else you need?" Fran asked. "I have another appointment at noon, so if you don't mind, I'll just scoot on out of here."

"No, I'm fine," he said as he thumped the papers. "Looks like I have what I need."

Elizabeth came in and got right to work. Jeremy was impressed with how Cindi and Elizabeth worked so well together. They both had the quiet confidence of people who enjoyed what they did and knew what they were doing. It made him wonder what else was going on to make Cindi put the shop on the market.

Since he had the rest of the day to himself, he decided to drive around and check out the changes to the place he'd called home all his life until he'd joined the army almost ten years ago. He drove through Sandy Springs, crossed the Chattahoochee River, and headed out on Johnson Ferry Road. New developments had sprung up, and the place was obviously thriving. It was a little too busy for his taste, but it still felt like home.

He drove all around Marietta and found his old house. It was much smaller and closer to the main road than he remembered. Many of the shops in downtown Marietta had changed, but it still had the flavor of old mixed with new.

By the time he headed back to his parents' condo, he was emotionally exhausted. Seeing things that brought back so many memories had worn him out. He looked forward to looking over Cindi's business figures and assessing the exact amount of success she'd had. She was obviously doing well, and now he'd know just how well.

"Have a good day, son?" his father asked during dinner.

"Pretty good. I think I've found a business to purchase."

"Oh yeah?" His dad put down his fork and leaned forward with interest. "What kind of business?"

There was no way to hedge, so he just came out with it. "A bridal shop."

His parents exchanged a look; then his father turned back to him. "Isn't that sort of a girlie business?"

Coming to his rescue, his mother said, "Not necessarily. Men get married, too."

"But a bridal shop sells wedding dresses for girls, right?"

"Well, yes," Jeremy replied, "but that really doesn't matter. I'm just in it for the business." He quickly looked down at his plate, trying to figure out a way to change the subject. He didn't want his parents to keep digging for information.

They'd always liked Cindi, and they didn't understand the breakup.

"I don't get it. Isn't there a more manly business you can buy—like a hardware store or something?"

❧

"I don't want someone to buy this place just to be an absentee owner," Cindi said. "I think I'll talk to Fran and tell her I can't sell to Jeremy since he doesn't even live here."

"I heard them talking, and he wasn't just looking to buy a business," Elizabeth said. "She's also trying to help him find a house."

"I don't care. I just can't see him running this place."

Elizabeth looked down then back up at her. "I understand what you're saying, but what I don't understand is why you care. I thought you were sick of the illusion of a happily-ever-after."

"I am."

"Then what's your problem? Why do you care who runs this shop if there's no happily-ever-after?"

Cindi sighed. "I don't know. It's just that I spend so much time coddling my customers and trying to make their wedding day special. Even if it doesn't last, don't you think brides at least deserve something special?"

Elizabeth clicked her tongue and shook her head. "I think you're confused."

"Maybe I am. My parents seemed perfectly happy all my life. I don't understand what happened. If they can't stick together, then who can?"

"It has nothing to do with your shop, Cindi. Maybe they were miserable all this time, but they stuck it out for you and your brother."

"Maybe so. I asked Mom how she could reconcile it with God. She hasn't even been to church since Dad left, ya know."

"That's very sad. How about your dad? I haven't heard you talk about him since he left."

Cindi lifted her head and snickered. "That's because I've only heard from him once since he left. He called me that one time, said he'd be in touch, then *poof*! He vanished."

"It's been what—two months? Give him time."

"I'm his daughter. You'd think he'd at least answer his cell phone when I called."

"What happened is awful, but I think you're taking it wrong. Maybe there's something you don't know about."

"Let's change the subject, okay?" Cindi said. "This is too upsetting."

"Whatever you want. Just remember I'm here, and I'm praying for you."

"Thanks," Cindi said with a forced smile. "We have an appointment in a half hour. Better put on our game faces."

The appointment was one of the few where the bride and her mother actually agreed. "We want to keep it simple," the daughter said. "I want something nice and understated."

Her mother nodded. "And there's a budget we have to watch very closely."

"No problem." Cindi was more than happy to accommodate people who were realistic and didn't have their heads in the clouds. She appreciated how up front these people were, so she worked hard to help them get the best they could afford.

"I have a sample dress that's on sale," Cindi said. "Elizabeth can alter it so it'll look custom-made."

"That would be wonderful," the mother-of-the-bride said with a smile.

The bride walked around the showroom and looked at not only bridal gowns but mother-of-the-bride dresses. "Do you have something on sale for my mother?"

Cindi studied the girl's mother then nodded. "I have several dresses I think she'd like. Do you prefer long or short?"

The bride liked the second dress she tried on, and her mother was excited she could afford to choose among three dresses. They left with smiles on their faces and a spring in their step.

After all the rejected dresses were put away, Elizabeth sighed. "Now that's how it's supposed to be."

"I agree. If the groom is as agreeable and nice as the bride's mother says he is, I have a feeling this will be a rare, wonderful union."

Cindi felt Elizabeth's scrutiny. Finally, Elizabeth cleared her throat. "Just think. If we weren't here and someone else was, they might not have been as happy. Someone else might have taken advantage of them and tried to sell them something they didn't want."

"Yes, I realize that."

"I wish you'd change your mind about selling, Cindi. You're the ideal person for this work. Ever since I can remember, you've wanted to work with brides."

Cindi shrugged. "That's all changed."

"So you're saying you didn't enjoy helping those people a few minutes ago?" Elizabeth tilted her head and studied her boss and friend.

"I didn't say that."

"Like I said, I think you're just very confused." As soon as she spoke her mind, Elizabeth took the pinned dresses to the back room to start on alterations.

A few minutes before closing time, the phone rang. It was Fran.

"I just heard from Jeremy," she said, her voice shrill with excitement. "He's ready to make an offer. When is a good time for me to present it? How about tomorrow?"

Cindi felt her heart drop. She dreaded this part but knew

she had to face it. "Tomorrow's fine. I get here at nine, and we open at ten."

"How about if I get there right after you? It won't take long."

"Okay, I'll see you then." Cindi dropped the phone back in the cradle and stared at the wall.

"What happened?" Elizabeth asked as she came around the corner.

"Fran's coming by first thing in the morning with an offer from Jeremy."

Elizabeth stood in silence for several seconds before speaking. "Do you plan to tell her then that you're not selling to Jeremy?"

Cindi backed away from her spot. "I'm not sure yet." She reached for her handbag and moved toward the door. "I need to leave now. Do you mind locking up?"

"Of course not. Do you want me here when Fran presents the offer?"

"No, but thanks. See you at ten tomorrow."

Streetlights twinkled in the dark as Cindi drove home. The shop stayed open late several nights each week to take care of working clients. She was tired, but she knew she wouldn't be able to rest much, knowing she was an inch away from selling the shop she'd dreamed about most of her life.

Between prayers for guidance, Cindi allowed herself to flash back to the times when she and Jeremy were together. It was high school, and they were kids. He'd moved from an apartment on the other side of Atlanta. He was so sweet and loving, she actually thought they might have a more lasting relationship than most high school romances. She'd heard rumors that he wasn't so wonderful from people who had friends from his old school. Apparently he'd started breaking girls' hearts back in middle school. He had a reputation for buying cheap trinkets and selling them for a hefty profit. Since she'd never seen that side of him, she assumed they were mistaken—and perhaps a little jealous.

He never had an interest in going to college, but that didn't matter to her. She was able to go because of her scholarship, but she'd entertained the thought that after college she'd come home to Jeremy and they'd be just as happy as they were in high school.

Now she had an offer on the shop—from the only guy she'd ever loved. She couldn't miss the irony of it all.

The next morning she got to the shop fifteen minutes before Fran showed up. "Hey there!" Fran said in a voice that was a tad too cheerful.

"Let's sit at the table," Cindi said, pointing to the consulting table.

Fran laid out some paperwork and turned a copy of the contract around to face Cindi. She went over each point and presented the offer. "Would you like to think about it?" she asked. "You have a couple of days."

Slowly, Cindi stood and shook her head. "No, I'm afraid I can't accept this offer."

Fran's smile quickly faded. "Why not?"

"I want my full asking price."

"Your asking price is a little steep, you have to admit," Fran said. "I assumed it was just a starting point so you'd have some room for negotiation."

Cindi cleared her throat and looked Fran in the eye. "It's not just the price. Jeremy and I have a past, and I really don't want to sell my shop to him."

Fran reached out and patted Cindi's hand. "I figured there was more to it than I realized. I can tell Jeremy is quite fond of you."

Cindi shrugged. "He's the one who dumped me."

"Perhaps there is more to it than meets the eye."

"I still don't want to sell to someone who doesn't understand a bride's needs during such an emotional time."

Fran offered a warm smile. "Jeremy has been very successful in business, so I think he'll figure it out."

"He was always an entrepreneur," Cindi said. "When I met him, he bought and sold concert T-shirts at school. He told me he started out in elementary school buying packs of gum and selling it on the playground, one stick at a time." She paused before adding, "And I heard he sold other stuff, too."

Fran let out a soft chuckle. "I'm not surprised. Jeremy is an intelligent man with a nose for what'll succeed."

"I'm not taking this offer," Cindi said firmly as she stood to end the conversation. "Sorry to waste your time."

"Oh, that's okay," Fran said as she gathered the papers. "It's all part of my job. This sort of thing happens all the time." She jabbered so quickly, Cindi could tell she was nervous. "I'll let Jeremy know, and I'm sure he'll come back with a counter to your counter." She paused. "You might want to let some of the past go, Cindi. . . . That is, if you really want to sell your shop."

Later that day, Fran called and said Jeremy had a counteroffer.

"What is it?" Cindi asked.

"Normally I don't do this over the phone, but I think you'll be pleased. He's offering your full price."

"Is he willing to run the shop?" Cindi asked.

"I talked to him about that and let him know how important that is to you. He said he'll run it, but not from there. He's talking about hiring someone to manage it on-site."

"I'm sorry, but I want the owner to actively manage my shop."

Fran started coughing but recovered quickly. "Don't you feel that's a little unreasonable?"

"No, not in this business. I've spent the last several years of my life making sure all the brides have gotten royal treatment. Their marriages might not last, but their weddings are important to them."

"You drive a hard bargain, Cindi."

"Maybe so, but I'm sticking to it."

Fran sighed. "Okay, I'll let him know."

Elizabeth was standing a few feet away and could obviously hear Cindi's part of the conversation, but she didn't say a word. Cindi was grateful her friend understood her enough to know when something wasn't open for discussion.

The next morning, about five minutes after she got to the shop, she watched Jeremy walk up to the door, try to open it, and knock when he realized it was locked. She let him in. He didn't offer a greeting or make small talk. Instead, he got right to the point.

"Cindi, I'd like to talk to you about your terms."

three

"Why are you turning down my perfectly good offers?" he persisted.

Cindi hadn't expected him to be so abrupt, so she took a step back. "I. . .uh. . ."

"You don't want to sell to me, do you?"

"It's not that," she said. "It's just that. . .well, I wanted someone to come in and be more hands-on."

"What makes you think I won't do that?" He widened his stance and folded his arms.

"Are you saying you've changed your mind?" she challenged.

He dropped the front. "Okay, so I'll be the first to admit I don't know a thing about running a bridal shop. That's why I'll hire someone to run it for me until I figure it out."

"That's not good enough. It needs to be run by someone who truly cares about making these women's most important day the best it can be."

She squirmed as he narrowed his gaze and studied her for several very long seconds. "Seriously, Cindi, why would it even matter? You clearly don't want to do this anymore, and I'm a willing buyer. Why don't you just sign on the line, and this shop will be my problem to deal with?"

"This shop is not a problem," she said more indignantly than she'd intended.

He shook his head. "This makes no sense to me."

"And that's precisely why I shouldn't sell it to you."

He lifted his hands in frustration and backed toward the door. "Whatever. I sure hope you get whatever it is you're looking for out of this deal. I thought it would be a win-win situation for both of us—a lucrative business for me and a way out for you to do whatever it is you wanted to do with your life."

His words stung much worse than she wanted him to know. She had to remain strong, though, as long as he stood in front of her.

"I'm sure you'll find other successful businesses that can make you the profit without having to be there," she said. "It's just not gonna be this one."

Jeremy was at the door already. He turned back to her before he left. "I'd like to discuss this further, but now isn't the right time for either of us. Just do me a favor and let me know before you sell to anyone else, okay?"

"Bye, Jeremy," Cindi said as she turned her back to him. She stood and waited until she was fairly certain he was gone. When the sounds of Atlanta traffic were muted by the closed door, she paused for a moment before turning around to face her shop.

&

Jeremy had no idea what had just happened. He'd been blindsided by her abrupt negativism toward him. Surely she'd gotten over their breakup from high school.

But had *he*?

His feelings toward her were as complicated as the business deal he couldn't seem to snag. He'd been turned down by many sellers, and it had never bothered him before. He just moved on and found something else.

Why was buying Cindi's Bridal Boutique so important to him?

Jeremy knew the answer without having to do much thinking. He wanted something of Cindi's simply to have a part of her. Giving her up so she could pursue her academic dreams had been difficult enough. The only reason he let her go was to give her the freedom she needed, but he couldn't tell her that.

He met Fran at the real estate office. She drove him around to different houses and condos, but none of them seemed right. Finally, she pulled over and turned to face him.

"What, exactly, do you want, Jeremy?"

Alarms went off in his head as he remembered wondering the exact same thing of Cindi. He sucked in a deep breath and blew it out in a long sigh.

Fran continued, "I have a feeling you know what you want, but you're trying to deny yourself. If you'll just say it out loud, maybe I can help you find it. I can see that you and Cindi have some unresolved issues. Care to talk about it?"

He snickered and shook his head. "Afraid it's not that easy. Tell you what. I'm really not in the mood to be looking at real estate today. Take me back to my car, and I'll call you when I won't be wasting your time."

"You're not wasting my time. This is my job. But I do want to help you find a nice place to live and a fabulous business that you can enjoy. Why don't we look at some other businesses? There are plenty in the book."

"Sounds good," he replied, "just not today."

He stopped off at the florist and picked up some flowers for his mother. Then he headed to a bookstore, where he found a simple question-and-answer book on the Bible so he could gently witness to his father. They'd been exceptionally good to him, and all he'd given them in return was one night out at a nice restaurant. It was the least he could do for the people who had loved him unconditionally all his life. Besides, he needed something to get his mind off Cindi Clark.

The instant he walked into the house, his dad greeted him. "How'd it go today, son?"

Jeremy took off his suit coat and draped it over the back of a living room chair. "Not so good. I haven't found the right business yet."

"Maybe you and your mother should think about opening a restaurant," his dad suggested. "With your business sense and her cooking talent, it would be a huge success."

Jeremy already had restaurants he was trying to sell. They were profitable, but they required too many hours. He wanted to pull everything in and settle down, but he didn't need to tell his parents that—not now, anyway. They'd worry something else might be wrong.

"Jeremy, would you mind giving me a hand in the kitchen?" his mother asked.

He was relieved to end the conversation with his father. He didn't want to have to explain anything about Cindi's bridal shop.

"How did your day go?" his mother asked once they sat down to eat.

Jeremy started to answer, but his dad stepped in. "He hasn't found his golden egg yet."

"Give him time." His mother grinned at him. "Our boy took his army talent and turned it into a gold mine."

"I was just a clerk in the army, Mom. All that did was give me time to think and help me grow up a little."

"It obviously did something good for you, son." His dad folded his napkin and placed it on the table. "You certainly didn't learn anything about business from us."

His mother immediately started clearing the table. "Why don't you two go watch the news while I clean up?"

Jeremy jumped up and took the plate from her. "I'll take care of that. Sit down."

She firmly held her ground. "We can clean the kitchen together." She slanted her gaze toward Jeremy's dad, who made a face but began to pitch in.

It took the three of them five minutes to carry everything into the kitchen and load the dishwasher. Afterward Jeremy said he was tired and needed to go to his room.

"Thanks for the flowers, sweetie," his mom said as she stood on her tiptoes and kissed him on the cheek. "You've always been good to me."

His dad followed him to his room. "Anything you want to talk about?"

Jeremy pondered the question for a few seconds then nodded. "Sure, Dad, come on in."

Once inside his room, he motioned for his dad to have a seat at his old desk while he sat on the edge of the bed. He pulled the package from the bookstore out of his bag and opened it. "You know, Dad, there's something I've always wondered about."

"What's that?" his dad asked as he glanced at the book Jeremy held.

"Why didn't you and Mom take us to church?"

His father hung his head and stared at the floor before looking back up at him. "We worked so hard just to put food on the table and keep you and your brother in clothes. Sundays were our only days off, and we needed the rest."

"I understand." And he did. "You know I've been going to church for several years now."

With a chuckle, his dad nodded. "That's another thing that puzzles me. You're a successful businessman who's gone and gotten religious."

Jeremy opened his mouth to explain the difference between his faith in God through Jesus and his father's perception of it being religious, but he needed to take this discussion slowly. He closed the book and handed it to his dad. "I picked this up for you at a Christian bookstore. It might explain some things better than I can."

A knock on the door brought Jeremy to his feet. "Mind if

I come in?" his mother asked.

"Sure, come on in. I was just about to tell Dad about today."

Jeremy started explaining that he thought the bridal business seemed extremely lucrative. "But the owner is digging her heels in because she doesn't think I can run it successfully."

His mom tilted her head to one side. "What's the name of the bridal shop?"

"Cindi's Bridal Boutique."

"Oh, now I understand." His mother nodded and smiled. "Cindi Clark owns that place."

After Jeremy explained more, his father gave him a perplexed look. "I still don't understand, son. What would you do with a bridal boutique?"

"It's a business, Dad."

"I'm sure it is to you," his mother interjected. "But it's really much more than that. I see Cindi's point. You don't know the first thing about what a bride wants or needs on her special day."

Jeremy groaned. "What's up with you women?"

His mother pointed her finger and shook it at him. "That kind of attitude is the very reason she's not selling it to you."

With a surrendering sigh, Jeremy slumped. "I'm sorry, Mom. I guess I just don't understand what the problem is. She wants to sell her shop, and I want to buy it. I've never seen this kind of resistance without a reason in business before. I've even offered her asking price, which is much higher than what it's worth."

"Have you stopped to think maybe it's not just a business to her? I remember Cindi. She's a very sweet girl. Maybe a little too romantic for her own good, but that's probably why she's so successful as a bridal shop owner. Did she say why she wants to sell?"

"She said she's ready to move on."

"That's not a good reason." His mother folded her hands

and looked pensively at them. "There has to be something else. Want me to find out?"

"No!" Jeremy and his father both said at the same time.

"Why not? It would be simple. I could just go into her shop and strike up a conversation with her."

"Mom, please don't. I wish I hadn't told you anything about it."

She stood up, a pained expression on her face. "Don't worry, I won't go near her if you don't want me to. But if you're serious about her. . .I mean about buying her shop, you should come right out and ask her why she's selling. And don't take her first answer, either."

"You don't understand," he said.

"I'm your mother. I understand much more than you think I do. Don't think I wasn't aware of how hard it was to let her go."

"Mom—"

She held up both hands to shush him. "I'm just saying that maybe the two of you need to sit down and have a heart-to-heart talk. Clear the air. Maybe then you'll find out what's going on with her."

Jeremy thought about what his mother had said, and she was right. This was the first time he'd ever had a hard time being rejected. It was obvious it wasn't because he wanted to be in the bridal business so badly—even to him.

He wanted to be near Cindi.

❧

The next morning Elizabeth was at the shop waiting for Cindi. "What're you doing here so early?" Cindi asked.

"I thought I'd unpack some of the accessory samples that came in yesterday."

"I have to finish entering the deposits, so I'll be at the computer until our first appointment."

"Cindi," Elizabeth said, then paused.

"Did you need something?"

"If you feel like talking, I'm all ears."

Cindi chuckled. "Thanks, but I really don't feel like talking. Sorry if I'm acting like a grouch."

"You're not a grouch, but I can tell you're bothered."

"It's just the shop. I wish someone would make a decent offer. Someone who cares as much as I do."

"I'm afraid that won't happen," Elizabeth said. "This shop is your baby. The only reason it's so successful is because of the time and energy you've put into it."

"With your help, of course," Cindi added.

"Yeah, well. . ."

Suddenly an idea dawned on Cindi. "Hey, it's really not a bad idea if you want to buy the shop. I can work out terms. I know you want to have children someday, but if you're in charge, you can bring the kids here."

"No thanks. I like working here, but I don't want what goes with owning a business. And Mike wouldn't want me to be away from home all those hours. You have to admit it can be pretty consuming."

"Good point."

"Besides," Elizabeth added, "without you here, it won't be as much fun."

Cindi glanced at the wall clock. "We have an appointment at eleven, so I need to get this work done."

"Who's the appointment?"

"Gail from church." Cindi pushed the power button on the monitor. "She wants to try on some bridal gowns and get color swatches for bridesmaid dresses."

"I'll get them ready," Elizabeth said as she disappeared around the corner.

At 10:55 the front door opened. Cindi grinned as she looked up, fully expecting to see Gail breezing in. But it wasn't

Gail. It was Jeremy.

He marched right up to where she stood, stopped, and looked at her. She frowned. "Did you forget something?"

"We need to talk, Cindi."

"Not now. I have an appointment in just a few minutes."

He didn't move an inch. "When will you be available?"

Cindi pushed away from the computer and came around from behind the desk. Jeremy followed her to the storage room, where she turned to face him. "Please, Jeremy, don't keep doing this. I don't want to sell my shop to you or any other absentee owner."

"What if I agree to work here—full-time?" he asked. "Will you sell it to me then?"

She laughed. "As if I actually believe you'd do something like that."

"Are you assuming things?"

"No." She knew she was scowling as she folded her arms, but she couldn't help it.

"Cindi!" Elizabeth called. "Gail's here."

"I'll be right there!" Cindi called back.

"Why don't I observe while you work with your customers?" he offered.

"Right."

"Seriously, Cindi. I'm very interested in what goes on here."

She turned at an angle as she thought about it. Five minutes with a future bride, and he'd run out of there screaming for mercy. "Fine. You're welcome to observe for a couple of days. But that still doesn't guarantee I'll sell the shop to you."

"Understood."

"When do you want to observe?"

He shrugged, palms up. "How about today?"

Cindi thought for a moment then nodded. "Remember Gail Rhodes, the music teacher?"

"Of course!" he replied. "I always liked Ms. Rhodes."

"She's out there waiting."

"Cool." Jeremy didn't wait for Cindi. He just turned around and headed out to the showroom.

The instant Gail spotted him, her face lit up with a huge smile. "Jeremy! What are you doing here?" Her smile was replaced by a puzzled expression as she looked at Cindi. "Are you two. . .well. . ."

"No, I'm just here to observe the business," Jeremy replied.

"I heard you were a business tycoon."

He chuckled. "I don't know about tycoon. I prefer to be called an entrepreneur."

"At any rate, welcome home." She turned back to Cindi. "Ready to make me a gorgeous, blushing bride?"

"The gorgeous part is easy because you already are, but I don't know about blushing," Cindi said.

"Yeah, it takes quite a bit to make me blush," Gail admitted. "I think I've seen everything."

"So who's the fortunate fella?" Jeremy asked.

"You probably don't know him. Isaac McClaury."

"Oh, I remember Coach McClaury. He was the coach of our biggest rival and the reason we lost our last game of the season. His team went on to win the league championship."

"Yep, that's him," Gail said. "He's still coaching."

"Well, congratulations," Jeremy said. "So when's the big day?"

Cindi cleared her throat. "I hate to interrupt, but we have a fitting to do, remember?"

Jeremy took a step back. "Sorry, I got carried away. I'll see you at church tomorrow."

"When did you start going to church?" The instant the words came out, Cindi regretted the way she said it. "Sorry, I didn't mean that the way it sounded."

"I understand," Jeremy said. "Look, why don't you do the

fitting, and we can talk about it later?"

Gail walked around the showroom picking out dresses, and Cindi made a few suggestions. Jeremy started to help, but he quickly backed away when Cindi glared at him. Elizabeth went into the fitting room to help Gail into the dresses while Cindi gathered some accessories to complement them.

"There's quite a bit more to this than I realized," Jeremy said as Cindi brushed past him.

"Well, yeah."

"You're extremely good at what you do, and you seem to enjoy it."

Cindi didn't respond; instead, she focused on gathering things for Gail. He was right. She loved what she did. But she couldn't help but remember the statistics on marriage. More than half of them would end in divorce, whether they bought dresses from her shop or not.

She got to the door of the fitting room, her arms full of tiaras, veils, undergarments, and a pair of shoes. Before opening the door, she turned to Jeremy. "Look, why don't we talk later?"

"When?"

"How about after work?"

He nodded and waved as he walked toward the door. "See you then."

As soon as he was gone, she knocked gently on the fitting room door. When Elizabeth opened it, she saw Gail standing on the platform, looking like a princess.

"You're absolutely gorgeous!" she said. "Here, try this tiara and veil. Are you wearing shoes?"

Gail lifted the front of the dress and stuck out her old brown clog. The three of them laughed.

"Now that's a wedding shoe original," Elizabeth said.

"I brought some great shoes for that dress." Cindi pulled the white satin pumps from the stack she'd placed on the floor. "All you have to do is step into them."

Once Gail had everything in place, she turned and got views from all sides. "Does anyone ever get the first dress they try?" she asked. "Because I absolutely love this one."

"Lots of girls do, but not until they try on other stuff," Cindi said. "I want to see you in more than one style."

Gail laughed. "You just want to confuse me. You know how I hate shopping."

"I know, but this is different. It's your wedding." She nearly choked on the words, and she didn't miss the knowing glance exchanged between Elizabeth and Gail.

"Okay, you're the expert." Gail sighed as she slipped out of the shoes and turned so Elizabeth could unzip the dress. "How about that one?" She pointed to a beaded, fitted gown they'd just received from a new designer. "I can't imagine liking anything more than this one, but I'll try on a few more."

Six dresses later, Gail pointed to the first dress. "I still like that one best. I'll bring the bridesmaids in for their fittings as soon as I decide on the color."

"Take your time," Cindi said. "It only takes a week to order the dresses, then another two weeks for alterations."

Gail took turns hugging Cindi and Elizabeth after she changed back into her regular clothes. "Thanks, both of y'all, for taking all this time with me. I'm much more relaxed now that I've found the perfect dress."

After she left, Elizabeth nodded. "We make a good team, don't we?"

A lump formed in Cindi's throat as she nodded. "The best."

The remainder of the day was busy with first appointments, final fittings, and paperwork. About five minutes before closing, Jeremy showed up. "Ready to talk?"

She nodded. "I'll be right with you. Let me close out of the computer."

"I'll stick around and lock up," Elizabeth said.

"Where do you want to go?" Jeremy asked.

"Let's just go for a walk."

"Sounds good."

Cindi was grateful Jeremy didn't jump right into negotiations for the shop. She needed to unwind before explaining anything.

"You look nice," Jeremy said as he looked her up and down. "You were always the prettiest girl I knew."

Cindi rolled her eyes. "That's not going to work, Jeremy. I've known you a long time."

He snickered. "It's true. You really are beautiful, but I understand."

They chatted for a few minutes. Jeremy started squirming, so Cindi assumed he was eager to discuss the business.

"Okay, let's get this over with," she said. "I think you need to let this opportunity go, because I'm not selling to you."

"Whoa. You sure are blunt."

"No, just honest."

"And you think I'm not?"

"I didn't say that." Cindi felt her stomach churning. "Look, Jeremy, I don't know why you came back or why you're so bent on buying my shop, but I don't want a confrontation."

"You still haven't given me a convincing reason you want to sell Cindi's Bridal Boutique."

"I didn't know I needed to convince you of anything."

"Touché."

"Sorry," she said. "I guess I'm a little touchy right now."

"You have every right to be. There's something I should probably tell you—something I was too immature to admit when we were kids."

"What's that?"

Cindi watched Jeremy's expression change as he gathered

his thoughts. "Back when we were together, I was happier than I've ever been. I loved you, Cindi, but I wasn't man enough to handle it."

"You don't have to do this." Cindi's voice cracked, so she cleared her throat.

"But I want to." She felt an odd sensation as he reached for her hand. "When you got that scholarship, I didn't want to stand in your way. I let you go so you could follow your dreams."

His admission sent a shock wave through her. She opened her mouth to speak, but nothing came out.

"A lot of time has passed since then. I just figured, well. . .I thought we'd be able to work this out somehow."

By the time they arrived back at the shop, Cindi had recovered enough to respond. "Look, Jeremy, I understand what you're doing, but I really don't think a bridal shop is what you want."

"Are you sure about that, or is it more a case of something you can't face?"

"Is that what you think?"

Jeremy closed his eyes for a couple of seconds before turning back to her with a softness in his expression she'd never seen before. "I'm thinking there are some things you're dealing with that you don't want to face."

"It's not about you, Jeremy." It annoyed her to no end that he'd gotten so close to the truth, but she wasn't ready to tell him about her parents.

Jeremy reached out and took her hand, gently stroking the back of it. She felt the chemistry between them again, but she couldn't deal with it. She stiffened, so he let go.

"If you need to talk, I'm all ears," he said softly as she stepped away.

If he only knew how close he'd come to her raw nerve.

four

Jeremy went to his car and stared after her, wondering what to do next. At this very moment he knew exactly what he wanted, and it wasn't her shop. It was Cindi.

Breaking up with her had been one of the most difficult things he'd ever done, but at the time he'd felt it was best for her. He couldn't help but wonder how different things would have been if he'd let their relationship take its course.

He'd always known she went to church a lot with her family, and he often wondered about it. She'd invited him, and he'd gone a few times. But he felt so out of place among people who understood the Bible that he found excuses to not return.

It wasn't until later, when one of his commanding officers in the army had witnessed to him and accepted the fact that Jeremy knew very little about the Bible, that he'd overcome his self-consciousness. Major Sharpe started by sharing short verses with explanations. When Jeremy had questions, the officer patiently answered all the ones he could and then admitted he didn't have all the answers. The chaplain was open and eager to share the gospel.

Hungry for the Word, Jeremy spent many hours studying his Bible and reading commentaries Major Sharpe and the chaplain recommended. After he got out of the army, he found a church close to where he lived. When he traveled, he chose whatever church was closest to his hotel, which gave him an interesting perspective on different ways to worship. Regardless of whether the services were contemporary or traditional, his favorite part of almost all services was the sermon, during which he never failed to pick up another rich morsel of God's greatness.

Jeremy had called one of his old high school buddies to find out where Cindi went to church these days. It didn't take his friend long to get back with him. She seemed surprised to hear he'd be there, and he couldn't blame her.

He went to his parents' house and put the breakfast dishes into the dishwasher before heading to his room. As much as the Atlanta area had changed, some things remained the same. Looking around at the posters on the walls, he realized his parents had moved everything from his old room to the condo. Knowing how sentimental his mother was, he figured she did it so he'd feel as though he'd never left. He removed his tie, loosened the top button on his shirt, and took off his shoes before lying on top of the comforter. It had been a long day.

When a knock came, he instantly sat up. "Mom?"

She opened the door a couple of inches. "You okay, Jeremy?"

"Sure," he replied as he stood, rolled up his shirtsleeves, and slid his feet into some loafers. "Need help setting the table?"

"No thanks, honey. Dinner is already on the table. You looked so tired, I didn't want to disturb you."

As he sat down with his parents to eat, he bowed his head and thanked the Lord for the meal. When he glanced up, he noticed his father looking at him curiously. Right when he started to witness, his mother asked him to pass the basket of biscuits; then his dad started talking about his day at work. He made a mental note to seize the next opportunity to talk about his faith as soon as he had an opening.

That night after dinner, his mother asked what his plans were for the weekend. "You've been so busy all week, I'd like to see you take it easy," she said.

"I plan to go to church." He paused as he watched for a reaction. "Wanna go with me?"

She crinkled her forehead and let out a nervous laugh. "Me in church? It's been so long, I'm not sure God would know who I am."

Jeremy chewed on his bottom lip as he searched for the right words. His mother studied him expectantly, so he reached out and touched her cheek. "Trust me, God knows who you are. He loves you."

She shook her head and looked away. "I don't know, Jeremy. It's been almost thirty years since I've stepped foot inside a church."

His heart ached at her admission, but he tried not to show how he felt. "Mom, I don't want to force you to do anything you're not comfortable with, but I'd love for you to go with me."

"I'll stick out like a sore thumb."

"No, you won't," he assured her. "I've been going to church ever since my last year in the army, and I've seen new people come in many times. It would make me happy to have you and Dad with me."

"I don't know about your father. You know how stubborn he can be."

Jeremy laughed. "I'm the most stubborn person I know, and I went."

Finally, she offered a slight smile. "Okay, you ask him."

"Then you'll go with me?"

She paused then nodded. "Yes, if your father agrees to go, but I have to go shopping for something nice to wear."

Jeremy's heart sang. He hadn't expected his mother to agree so quickly. Now all he had to do was talk to his father.

After she left, he approached his father, who'd settled into his recliner with the remote control in his hand. "Dad, can we talk for a minute?"

"Sure, son." He put the TV on mute then turned to Jeremy. "Whatcha got on your mind?"

"I'm going to church on Sunday, and I'd like for you and Mom to go with me."

"I've never been much of a churchgoer," his dad said.

"I wasn't, either, but now I am."

"Yeah, but that's different. You're much younger than me. It's easier for you to adapt." He turned back to stare at the silent TV.

Jeremy didn't want to jump on any argument, so he let a little bit of time elapse before making his case. "It wasn't easy the first time I went. In fact, I was scared to death that either I'd be rejected by God or someone from the church would point their finger at me and let everyone know I didn't belong there."

His dad pursed his lips then turned to face him. "I'd feel like a foreigner in church. I wouldn't know what to do or how to act."

Rather than argue that no one had to act, Jeremy chose to take a different approach. "I'll be there. If you need to know something, I'll tell you."

He saw how difficult it was for his dad to talk about church, but that was okay. Sometimes things were better if they weren't easy.

"Can I let you know tomorrow? I need to think about it."

"Sure." Jeremy stood and took a few steps before turning back to face his dad, who still had the TV on mute. "By the way, Mom said she'll go if you do."

Jeremy knew that would get him, even if not immediately. He smiled, offered a clipped nod, and turned toward the guest room. "I think I'll head to my room now. I'd like to study some business figures and then read my Bible."

As soon as Jeremy got to his room, he closed the door and leaned against it. His love for Christ had become his driving force, which was the reason he wanted to unload some of his businesses and settle near his parents. With so many things pulling him in so many different directions, he felt the distractions weren't healthy for him spiritually. He needed the calm serenity of home—a place where he could hoist an anchor and feel the love of friends from church and be near family.

He understood his parents' reluctance to go with him, but he wasn't going to give up on his call to share his faith. When he'd first thought about it, he imagined his father being more resistant than he was. He was surprised he hadn't gotten a resounding *no*.

The Lord had gently nudged Jeremy back to Marietta. Shortly after he'd decided it was time to settle down, he'd spoken to his mother, who assumed he meant he was coming home. He didn't have the heart to tell her he hadn't decided exactly where he wanted to settle, and since the Atlanta area had been his home for the first nineteen years of his life, he figured why not go back? And here he was.

※

Sunday morning Cindi stood in front of her full-length mirror and turned to the side. She'd put a couple of pounds on lately, so the skirt didn't hang right. With a sigh of frustration, she changed into a dress that hid her midriff bulges. She was still petite, but she wouldn't be for long if she wasn't careful. How did Elizabeth get away with not putting on an ounce after eating nonstop cake, ice cream, brownies, and anything else she wanted, while one fattening meal was all it took for Cindi's silhouette to change completely? She'd had this problem all her life. Her mother once told her it was genetic—that she was supposed to have a little extra meat on her bones.

After she finally found an outfit that didn't make her look as though she'd been stuffing herself with marshmallows, she left for church. Elizabeth always saved her a seat near the front on the right-hand side.

She arrived just a few minutes before the service was due to start, so she quickly parked her car, hopped out, and ran up the church steps. She was focused on getting to her seat. When she heard her name, she turned to see who was calling her.

There was Jeremy, standing between two people. She would have recognized his mother, but his dad was shorter and thinner than she remembered.

"Why, Cindi Clark, you sure have grown into quite a young woman," Mrs. Hayden said. "Isn't she lovely, Jeremy?"

Jeremy grinned at her. "Yes, very lovely."

"Thank you. It's nice to see y'all." Cindi was at a loss for words, but she didn't want to be rude.

Mr. Hayden looked uncomfortable in his dark suit and tie. "Nice to see you, too," he said as he shifted from one foot to the other.

Cindi glanced around as people filed past her. "Why don't you come on in and find a good seat? I'm supposed to meet Elizabeth in our regular place. We always sit together since her husband is in the choir. Maybe there are a few extra seats nearby."

"Oh, go on, then," Mrs. Hayden said as she waved her away. "We'll be fine."

Jeremy nodded. "Thanks anyway. See you tomorrow."

"Um. . .okay." Cindi turned and scurried into the church toward Elizabeth, who had turned completely around to watch.

"Was that Jeremy I saw you talking to?" Elizabeth asked as soon as Cindi plopped down on the seat next to her.

"Yep."

"Who are the people with him?"

"His parents."

"Did you expect to see them here?" Elizabeth asked.

"Jeremy wasn't that much of a surprise, but I've come to expect the unexpected with him. However, I never thought I'd see his parents in a church. They never went when he was growing up."

Elizabeth smiled at her. "The Lord is amazing, isn't He?"

Throughout the service, Cindi couldn't get her mind off the fact that Jeremy was somewhere in the building. At first she marveled at the miracle of his parents being there. Then she wondered why he'd chosen this particular church to bring them to. She even thought perhaps he was using church for business purposes. By the time the service was over, anger had swelled inside her at the notion that he might be using church to get her to sell him the bridal shop.

As soon as the last worship song was sung, Elizabeth stood and turned around. "I see them."

"Who?" Cindi asked.

"Jeremy and his folks. They're over by the exit."

❧

Jeremy glanced at his parents, who remained seated next to him. They didn't seem so uncomfortable now.

"Well, son, would you like to go out for lunch?" his dad asked as people filed past them.

His mother laughed. "Just like you to always be thinking about your next meal."

"Isn't that what you're supposed to do? Leave church and pack the restaurants?" Jeremy laughed at his dad's deadpan tone.

"Why don't we head over to the Old Hickory House?" Jeremy said as he stood and gestured for his parents to do the same. "I'm in the mood for some biscuits and country ham."

He glanced over his shoulder in time to see Elizabeth looking directly at him. When their gazes met, she flashed a wide smile and waved. He waved back then turned to leave.

As he ushered his folks out the door, he thought about how Cindi had acted toward him. He decided to work harder at getting to know her again.

He helped his parents into his dad's car then went around and got behind the wheel. "My treat."

His dad nodded. "Sounds good."

Old Hickory House was crowded, but the host seated them within half an hour. Once the waitress took their order, his mother turned to him. "Church was very nice."

Jeremy looked at his dad. "Did you enjoy it, too?"

His dad lifted a hand to his mouth and coughed. "It was okay."

That was as good as he expected. "Since I'm moving back to the Atlanta area, I need to find a church home. I figured we'd start there and go to different places each Sunday."

"Why look at other churches when that one is just fine?" his dad asked.

That caught Jeremy by surprise. "So you actually liked it?"

"Like I said, it was okay. . .for church."

Jeremy couldn't resist probing deeper. "What, exactly, do you mean by that?"

"The sermon was interesting, and the music sounded good."

His mother tapped her finger on the side of her chin. "Did you know Cindi would be there?"

Leave it to her to be so direct. He wasn't about to lie.

"Yes."

She narrowed her eyes and studied him. "I still think there's something between you two—besides you trying to buy her shop. I saw how the two of you looked at each other."

Jeremy looked down at the table as he hesitated, then figured he might as well level with his parents. "There's some unfinished business between us."

"I thought so," his mom said. "It's been a long time, so don't get your hopes up."

"Trust me. I've dealt with disappointment many times. I can handle it."

Their food arrived, so their conversation turned to how much he'd missed the Old Hickory House biscuits. His mother kept giving him a look that let him know she was concerned about him. He wasn't sure if hinting at his feelings toward Cindi had been a good idea, but it was too late to worry about that now.

They were almost finished with their meal when his mother looked him squarely in the eye. "Jeremy, rather than let her think all you care about is her business, why don't you just level with her? I think it would be easier to start your own business from scratch—something more suitable for a young man than a bridal shop—than to chase after hers if what you really want is her."

He started to tell her that was exactly what he planned to do, but he didn't. "You're right as usual," he said with a smile. "That's what I'll do."

"Sure you will," she retorted. "I've known you all your life, and you've never given up if there's something you really want."

The next morning he awoke with a new plan. He'd stop off and visit Cindi to let her know his new business plans. While he was at it, he might just see what he could do to rekindle their relationship. The more he thought about the prospect of being with Cindi again, the more determined he was.

His mother grabbed him before he got out the door. "I have something I almost forgot about. I remembered after church, but by the time we got home, it slipped my mind again."

"What's that?"

"Go look in the shoe box on the table."

After a quick peek inside, he smiled. His mother had just

given him an opening with Cindi. "Thanks, Mom. Mind if I take it?"

"Go ahead. It's yours. I was just holding on to it for safekeeping."

When he pulled up in front of the bridal shop a few minutes before it was due to open, he saw someone was already inside with the lights on. He paused, said a prayer, then got out to see if Cindi would give him the time of day.

He watched Cindi through the glass door as he approached. As soon as she <u>heard</u> someone enter, she glanced up with a bright smile. When she realized it was him, her expression instantly changed.

five

The first flutter of excitement at seeing Jeremy faded to annoyance. What was he doing here so early? Did he think being here would change anything?

"Good morning," he said as he thrust a shoe box toward her. "My mother found this in my old room. Thought you might like to see it."

Cindi glanced at the box. "What is it?"

He put it on the counter. "See for yourself. Go ahead and open it."

She cautiously lifted the lid and glanced in the box. Inside was a nice neat stack of pictures that had been carefully layered between tissue. The top picture was a duplicate of one she had stuck away in an old photo album and avoided for years.

"You kept all these?" she asked as she lifted the one that was a duplicate of hers. "We really went all out for prom, didn't we?"

He laughed. "I remember how nervous I was. My mother helped me pick out your corsage, and my dad had to help me with my tie because my hands were shaking so much."

Cindi thumbed through the stack before putting the lid back on top. "I'm surprised you still have these."

He tilted his head. "Why?"

"I never thought you were the sentimental type."

Jeremy stood there in silence for a few seconds while Cindi watched. Finally, he shook his head.

"To be honest, I'd forgotten about them. These were at my

parents' house. My mom gave them to me this morning."

"Oh, so you weren't holding on to them. Your mother was." Unexpected disappointment flooded her. "That's sweet of her."

"Yes, very sweet." He remained standing there, watching. . . waiting.

"Thanks for the nostalgic moment, Jeremy, but I have work to do."

"I'm not stopping you."

"Look, Jeremy, I think I know what you're doing, but it's not going to work. I don't know how many times I have to tell you I'm not selling my business to anyone who doesn't care about brides."

He tilted his head forward and set his jaw, holding her gaze for a couple of seconds before she averted her attention to the piece of paper on the counter. She was almost certain he could hear her heart pounding, so she reached over and turned on some music.

She felt her cheeks grow hot as he continued standing there staring at her. Had he sensed her pounding heart and her yearning for the same feeling she'd had as a hopeful teenage girl?

As abruptly as he'd arrived, he backed toward the door. Her muscles gradually relaxed when he was across the room.

"I'm not giving up, Cindi—but I'm not talking about business now."

She tilted her head with a puzzled expression. "Then what are you talking about?"

"We used to be good together, and I still think there's a chance for us."

Had she just heard him correctly? "You're kidding, right?"

"Nope. I'm as serious as I've ever been." He took a step backward. "I don't give up easily, so you might as well get used to seeing me around."

As soon as he was gone, Cindi's knees weakened, so she lowered herself into the chair by the counter. She bowed her head in prayer for the strength to withstand anything Jeremy said or did. He'd gotten to her years ago, and he was getting to her now.

"Hey, girl, are you okay?"

Cindi jumped. "How did you get in here without me hearing you come in?"

Elizabeth shrugged. "I dunno. I thought you were asleep." She leaned over and looked Cindi in the eye. "You look like you don't feel well."

"I'm okay, just a little rattled."

"Jeremy?" Elizabeth went around behind the counter and pulled out her appointment book.

Rather than deny the obvious, Cindi just nodded. "He's been here already this morning. The man simply won't give up."

Elizabeth's glance darted toward the box Jeremy had left on the counter. "What's this?"

"Go ahead. Open it and see for yourself."

Elizabeth lifted the lid and looked inside. "Whoa."

"His mother kept those all these years, so he thought I needed to see them."

"As if you didn't already have your own pictures." She'd pulled out the whole stack and started studying each one.

"Hey, I'm in this one."

Cindi joined Elizabeth behind the counter. "Let's see."

They spent the next several minutes going through the pictures and recalling the events. "It's amazing how something like this can make the memories so clear—it's almost like it happened yesterday," Elizabeth said. "Look. This one was taken at the Varsity after we won the last football game of the season."

"Yes, I remember," Cindi replied softly. In fact, she even remembered what she ordered that night, but she wasn't about to share that. The whole evening was vivid in her mind because that was the night Jeremy had told her he loved her.

Elizabeth belted out a hearty chuckle. "Look at this one. Remember when we all piled into that new guy's car and headed out for Macon? We'd gotten halfway there when you suddenly remembered you had to be home early."

How could Cindi have forgotten? She was embarrassed she had an early curfew that night, so she didn't say anything right away. But when she did, Jeremy didn't hesitate to make sure she got home on time. He'd been such a gentleman before he suddenly. . .

"Are you okay?" Elizabeth asked.

Tears stung the back of Cindi's eyes as she nodded. "I'm fine. I just need to concentrate on business right now."

Elizabeth put the pictures back into the box, lifted it from the counter, and stuck it in a cubbyhole. "I understand." She flipped open the appointment book. "Let's see. . .we have one appointment this morning for a final fitting, then three brand-new brides coming in back-to-back."

The phone rang, signaling their busy day had begun. Cindi welcomed the pace, but with each new bride she helped, she wondered how the marriage would work out. Would the bride still be happy a year later? Would her husband continue to be as attentive as he was during the dating period and the honeymoon? The statistics were downright heartbreaking.

Cindi had mixed feelings at closing time. She was exhausted, but without the steady stream of customers to assist and vendors to contact, she had to face her own thoughts.

She'd just locked the shop door when Jeremy pulled up in front of her and lowered his window. "It's a nice night. Want to go for a drive?" he asked.

A lump formed in her throat. She slowly shook her head. "I really need to go home, Jeremy."

"And do what?" he asked.

She wanted to tell him it was none of his business—that her time was her own and she needed that time away from him. All he did was muddy her thoughts. But she couldn't. Her will wasn't strong enough to resist talking to the man who had her emotions swirling among her confused thoughts.

"I really don't have specific plans." She shrugged. "But I had a busy day, and I'm tired."

"Then hop in and you can tell me all about it."

She squinted and stared at him for a few seconds. Was he serious, or was he being sarcastic?

There didn't appear to be any mischief in his expression. In fact, he looked hopeful.

He continued watching her as she mulled over the thought of being with him. Her initial reaction was *no way*. But seeing the pictures had brought out something in her that she hadn't felt in years—since she'd last been with him—and she sort of enjoyed the feeling.

Finally, she nodded. "Okay, but I can't stay out late."

"Want me to follow you home and leave from there, or do you want me to take you back to your car here?"

She shook her head as she tried to organize her thoughts. It was time to be direct. "Why don't you just follow me home? My place isn't too far away."

He smiled. "I know."

⁊

It didn't take long to get to her place. She pulled into the driveway, and he was right behind her. As soon as she got in his car, he turned to her. "We really need to talk about what happened. I was such an idiot for how I handled myself when we were kids."

He watched her expression change from surprise to resignation. "That's just it, Jeremy. We were kids. It was just a high school crush."

"Oh, I think there was more to it than that," he replied. "And I believe, deep down, you agree with me."

"I don't think it'll work, Jeremy," Cindi said as she tried to look everywhere but at him. "It's been a long time."

"Can we at least give it a shot?"

When she glanced at him, he felt a surge of emotion he had to fight to keep down.

"I don't know. I'm so busy, and my life is exactly how I like it."

That raised another question. "Then why are you selling your shop?"

Cindi closed her eyes momentarily then opened them. She looked him in the eye and said, "I don't believe in what I do anymore."

"You what?" That was an answer he hadn't expected.

"Ever since my parents split up, I realized all I'm doing is trying to peddle a fairy-tale life that doesn't exist."

"Your parents split?" He couldn't imagine how he'd feel if that happened to him. "They always seemed fine to me."

She snorted. "They seemed fine to everyone, including me, which is why it was such a shock. When I first started my business, I imagined all marriages being as wonderful as my parents'. When brides came to me looking for a dress, I spent time helping them pick out the perfect gown to wear as they walked toward their life partner. After I was open a year, one of the brides came in to tell me she was getting a divorce. That shocked me. And I felt bad that I'd been part of an illusion. But at least then I had my parents' marriage to hold up as a model."

"People get divorced, Cindi. It had nothing to do with you."

"I know."

As he watched her wince, he felt an overwhelming grief at how her dream had shattered.

"But it still hurt. Then I found out about other bridal customers whose marriages hadn't worked out."

"Okay, so some of your brides divorce, and your parents have split. That's going to happen. Granted, it's an awful thing, but you can't control what happens to other people after you do your job."

"You're right," she agreed, "but I can stop playing the game of happily-ever-after when it's nothing but an illusion."

Oh, she's really hurting. He wanted to reach out and comfort her—to touch her cheek and feel the softness of her skin.

She offered a forced smile. "So that's why I'm selling my business."

"Let me get this straight," he said as he carefully chose his words. "You don't believe in marriage anymore, so you're selling your very profitable bridal shop."

"Right."

"Then why does it matter what the new owner does with it—whether the person is hands-on or an absentee owner?"

"I know this probably doesn't make sense, but I still care."

"It does make sense," he replied. "I've known you for a very long time, Cindi Clark. You care about everything. Sometimes too much for your own good." He paused to smile, and he was delighted that she grinned right back at him. "You're a sweet, honest, caring woman who doesn't want any part of less than the best."

She glanced down then shyly looked back at him. "Thanks."

"I mean every word of it, too."

"Good. Now are we going for a drive, or did you just want to sit here?"

He snickered. "I was so caught up in the conversation, I forgot." He put the car in reverse. "So what do you plan to do after you sell your business?"

"I have no idea." She blinked a couple of times before

grinning. "Okay, now it's my turn. Why did you come back to Marietta?"

"Good question." He took a moment to decide whether or not to let her know the real reason versus the shorter version he reserved for when he didn't feel like talking. He chose the latter. "I've been feeling sort of nostalgic for my family, and my parents aren't getting any younger."

"Your parents look pretty good to me."

"Yes, they do, don't they?" he agreed. "That's not all. I felt like I needed to make amends with you after the way I botched the best relationship I ever had."

"Jeremy." Her voice held a warning tone.

He pulled off the road into a parking lot and put the car in park before turning to face her. "You do understand the reason I broke up with you that night, don't you?"

She closed her eyes and folded her arms. With a heavy heart, he unfastened his seat belt, scooted closer to her, and gently put his arm around her. At first she stiffened, but she gradually relaxed. However, she didn't lean into him the way she did back in high school.

He reached over and turned her chin so she was facing him. "I never stopped loving you, Cindi. I figured since I wasn't going to college, I needed to let you go so you could fulfill your dreams."

She frowned. "So you're saying you did it for me?"

He nodded.

She pulled away. "I don't buy that, Jeremy."

She might as well have sprayed him with water then tossed a load of bricks at him. He took a deep breath and slowly let it out. He'd hurt her more than he realized. He needed to give her a little space and let things happen more naturally.

"Hey, let's lighten up a bit," he said. "Why don't you fill me in on what everyone is doing?"

She looked at him with suspicion, but she took the question and ran with it. He enjoyed watching her as she told him about several of their old high school friends, letting him know who was doing what and where they were. He wanted to know more about her family, but after her revelation about her parents, he wasn't about to go there—at least not now.

Finally, she pointed to the road. "I really need to get home now, Jeremy. I have a long day tomorrow, and I haven't eaten yet."

"We can grab something if you want."

She offered him a smile. "Thanks, but I'll just get something at home."

"I'd like to get together again. This was fun."

She didn't respond directly to his comment. She waited until they got to her driveway. "Thanks for explaining things."

Being with Cindi brought back memories and gave him a different perspective of who he was. His business dealings since he'd left town had been cold and calculating. Now he had to do things differently. He had to be softer. Gentler. In a way, even coddle her. But he couldn't be the least bit condescending. He didn't want her to think he was interested in anything but her.

⋆

The rest of the evening Cindi's thoughts vacillated between how Jeremy made her feel and whether selling her business was such a good idea. When she'd listed it with Fran, she figured some stranger—some woman she didn't know— would come in and fall in love with running a bridal shop. Cindi thought she'd teach the basics of running this sort of nurturing business to a person who'd never done it before. At first when she turned Jeremy down, she thought she was protecting her business from someone who didn't care about it. However, now that he'd backed off, she knew she was protecting her heart.

This was insane! She could have dreamed all day of how things would go, and this scenario never would have crossed her mind. Being with him had opened the floodgate of memories that brought her back to a time in her life when she was innocent and naive.

Being naive at this point in her life wasn't an option. However, she'd maintained her innocence to keep from giving in to the ways of the world. After losing Jeremy years ago, Cindi had held out hope that one day she'd meet a great guy who loved the Lord as much as she did. Until then, she'd keep running her shop and being there for young women who'd found their Prince Charming.

Even after announcing they were separating, her mother had tried to talk her into keeping her shop. "This is what you've wanted all your life. Don't give up on your dream," her mother had said.

But how could she hang on to a dream that involved something that didn't exist? Everlasting love. Unconditional love. The type of love the Lord wanted for His followers. It was the idea the Lord had designed but the world had scorned.

Her parents had always gone to church and brought her and her brother to church, yet they'd still decided to go their separate ways. No amount of explaining would justify how that could happen.

"What do you plan to do once the shop sells?" her mother had asked.

Cindi had no idea. Her business degree had given her the basic knowledge she needed for the shop, but it was too general to give her any specific idea for later. For the first time in her life, she was acting out of character and doing something on impulse. She knew she needed a plan, but since all she'd ever wanted was to be in the bridal business, nothing had come to mind.

During the next several days, business was steady, but nothing major happened. Every day they had new brides-to-be coming in with stars in their eyes, and it took everything Cindi had not to squelch their enthusiasm.

"Where's Jeremy?" Elizabeth asked when they hadn't seen him in a week.

Cindi shrugged. "I guess he finally got the hint."

&

Jeremy had been called to Savannah, where he closed on a couple of restaurants and a tour business near downtown. He'd been trying to sell all of them, but the market had been soft until recently, so he was glad to be done with them. Even though he had someone running the places, there was always the risk of having to go back.

Now that he had them off his mind, he could concentrate on what he really wanted—Cindi. Because of Cindi's reluctance to sell to him, he had to figure out a different excuse to come around.

He left behind what had been his favorite businesses when he'd decided to return to Atlanta. As much as he loved being a part of people experiencing the dolphin cruise and a carriage ride through the old part of town followed by a good old-fashioned Southern meal, he was ready to settle into a new life—one that involved being immersed in church and his family. He wished Cindi was part of that equation, but unless something major happened, he didn't see that in his near future.

After he finished his business in Savannah, he let out a sigh of relief. When he reached the parking lot of his parents' condo, he sat in his car and stared at the dashboard. He knew there would be questions he wasn't in the mood to answer as soon as he went inside. His bank account was padded with the proceeds of the businesses, so at least he could go looking for a place of his own now. He loved his folks, but he needed his own space.

To his surprise, his mother greeted him with nothing more than a hug and a kiss on the cheek. "I cooked spaghetti for supper, and I put the leftovers in the refrigerator if you want to heat them up in the microwave."

His dad had already gone to bed, so he thanked his mother and fixed himself a quick dinner before going to the guest room. Once there he made a list of things to do the next day, which included a brief stopover at Cindi's shop.

He got there before she did the next morning and was waiting for her by the front door.

"What're you doing here so early?" she asked.

"You didn't think I'd give up, did you?"

After she rolled her eyes, Cindi unlocked the door and stepped inside. Jeremy followed right behind her.

She glanced over her shoulder. "Would you mind flipping the light switch by the door?"

He reached over and did as he was told. She still hadn't commented on the flowers in his hand, but he'd seen her glance at them.

After she had everything set up and turned on, she walked over to him. "I've been thinking about our talk the other night. Maybe it's not such a good idea for you to keep coming around."

"Cindi," he said softly, taking a step toward her. "I'd really like us to get to know each other better. As adults. I want you to see me in a different light."

"You know how I feel, Jeremy."

"No, I really don't. All I know is that ever since I've come to Christ, my whole perspective has changed. I feel I've been led here, and I'm not about to turn back now."

"But—" She paused and widened her eyes. "Stop it right now, Jeremy. Whatever you're up to isn't right for me."

❧

He'd mentioned his new faith in Christ, but how could she tell if he was being honest with her? All she knew for certain was that he'd stop at nothing to get what he wanted. He'd started out wanting her business and finally seemed to give up on that, so he must not have wanted it all that badly. Either that or he had a new tactic that involved a bluff. After the pain he'd caused so many years ago, how could she trust that he wasn't pursuing her business through her heart?

six

She had to turn away quickly or she feared she might buckle under the temptation to get emotional about Jeremy. Old feelings flooded her.

"Like I told you, we have some unfinished business," he added.

She squared her shoulders and looked him directly in the eyes. "The only business I have is this one, and I need to get back to work."

Jeremy glanced down at the floor and sighed. He looked sad, but she wasn't sure if it was sincere or part of an act. Whatever the case, she needed him to leave.

"Okay, I'll go now. But you need to understand I don't give up easily." He took a step toward the door, pivoted to face her, and added, "On anything."

Elizabeth came in as he walked out the door. She lifted an eyebrow. "Looks like a man on a mission."

"Yes, I'm afraid so," Cindi agreed. "He says he's not going to give up."

"Just remember how he broke your heart back in high school. I'm not saying he hasn't changed, but be careful, okay? I've always thought Jeremy was charming, but I don't want to see you get hurt again."

Cindi pulled out the two appointment books and handed Elizabeth's to her. "Yes, of course." She flipped hers open. "I have back-to-back appointments until about three. You have a final fitting at ten; then I need your help. My eleven o'clock is the entire wedding party."

"Is this the Myers group?"

"That's the one," Cindi said with a snicker. "I told Lynda she needed to give me a final count on the number of bridesmaids, but she keeps adding them."

"How many is she up to now?"

Cindi pulled out the Myers file and glanced at her notes. "Last I checked, eleven."

Elizabeth shrugged. "She might as well make it a dozen."

"Yeah, why not? It's good for business, right?"

Elizabeth glanced up from her appointment book and studied Cindi. "You sound cynical."

"I can't help it with all the broken hearts and shattered dreams in the world today. Weddings aren't what they used to be. I know I sound like a broken record, but I remember thinking it was a wonderful celebration with family and friends witnessing the union of two people before God—promising to love and respect each other until the end."

"That's still what it's supposed to be," Elizabeth reminded her. "Are you okay? I can handle everything if you need to go home."

Cindi shook her head. "No, I'm fine. I guess I just needed to vent. Let's set up for the first appointment. The bride said she wants something simple. It's a church wedding, and she only has two bridesmaids. Her father is deceased, and her mother is walking her down the aisle."

The discussion quickly turned to what they'd show the bride and her mother. Cindi was relieved they'd moved on from talking about Jeremy, who'd taken over most of her thoughts when she wasn't at work.

The first appointment didn't take long. As soon as the bride tried on her third dress, she made her decision. "I've never been much of a shopper," she said. "This is what I want, so there's no point in trying on more." She picked the dresses for her two bridesmaids then left.

"She must not be from the South," Elizabeth quipped.

Cindi laughed. Leave it to Elizabeth to crack a joke like that. "Actually, she's from Macon."

"I bet her parents are from up North."

The next appointment took almost three hours, causing Cindi and Elizabeth to skip lunch. They had to take turns working with a conflicting appointment to keep from backing up the rest of their schedule.

By late afternoon, they were exhausted. "One more bridal party this afternoon; then we can coast," Elizabeth commented.

The next day, they both arrived at the shop at the same time. Elizabeth had to work on alterations, while Cindi needed to prepare for the day's appointments. They both looked over their schedules and worked up a plan to handle all their tasks.

Then Jeremy walked in. Elizabeth took that opportunity to go to the sewing room. "If you need me, I'll be in there," she said.

"So," Jeremy said when they were alone, "is there any way I can convince you to go out with me tonight?"

He obviously meant what he said when he told her he wouldn't take no for an answer. "You really don't give up, do you?"

"Not often," he admitted.

"Tell you what," Cindi finally said. "Maybe later. I'm busy today."

He lifted his hand in a wave and moved toward the door. "At least you didn't say no this time. See you soon."

As soon as he left the shop, Cindi headed straight for the sewing room. "I can't believe the nerve," she growled.

"Um, what did you expect? He's obviously a man in love."

Cindi narrowed her eyes. "Whose side are you on, anyway?"

"I don't have to give up my romantic outlook just because you've become cynical."

"True." Cindi moved a few things around on the counter for something to do with her hands. "Just don't get those romantic notions about Jeremy and me."

"Sometimes I think he's changed, but I agree. You were hurt too badly to go there again. No point in taking any chances."

"We've both seen him at church. I think he's changed," Cindi admitted, "at least a little."

"Don't get me wrong," Elizabeth continued as she closed the gap between them. "I like Jeremy. Deep down, I think he's basically a good guy. It's just that there's an edge to him that we'll never understand."

"That's probably why he's been so good in business."

"Don't forget you have one of the most successful bridal shops in the Southeast. You're good in business, too."

"I'm sure some people would argue that point."

"You can't control what other people think, Cindi. This shop means a lot to you, no matter what you say. Even now. Look at you." Elizabeth gestured toward her. "The very thought of someone coming in here and doing anything to hurt what you've built has you in a total tizzy." She paused then asked, "Have you figured out what you'll do once you sell?"

Cindi didn't want to think that far into the future, so she avoided answering the question directly. "So you think I'm making a mistake?"

Elizabeth tilted her head and offered a pitying look. "I don't want to tell you what to do."

"I'm not saying I want you to tell me what to do. All I'm asking—"

A walk-in customer arrived, cutting their conversation short. The rest of the day was busy, so they didn't have another chance to talk.

After work Cindi went to her car and found a note stuck to the window. She didn't have to look at it to know whom it was from; his handwriting hadn't changed since high school.

Cindi, give me a call after you get home. Here's my cell phone number: 555-3738. Love, Jeremy.

She started to crumple it up but changed her mind. She folded it instead and dropped it into her purse. She'd decide later if she should call. After dinner.

Cindi made a stop at Publix for some quick and easy food from the deli, then headed home. Her stomach growled and her head ached. It had been a very long day.

As soon as she got inside, she kicked off her shoes and headed straight for the kitchen, where she dropped the grocery bags and her purse. Most of the time she turned on the TV to watch the news while she ate, but not tonight. She had some serious thinking to do.

She prepared a plate, carried it to the table, sat down, and said her blessing. The food tasted good, but after a couple of bites her stomach ached from anxiety.

Elizabeth had challenged her decision and given her quite a bit to think about. And now Jeremy wanted her to call. She felt torn. There were so many angles she hadn't thought of when she'd abruptly put her shop on the market. With each new event, she realized her issues were deeper than she'd originally thought.

As an adult child of newly separated parents, Cindi still had a hard time getting over feeling betrayed. How long had they been thinking about splitting? Was there anything she could have done to keep them together? Her brother had long since been gone, and when she'd contacted him with the news, he didn't even offer to come home. His techie job was demanding and he was up for a promotion, so he couldn't come home to help her talk some sense into their parents. That bugged her, but she couldn't control him. So she'd set out to talk to them on her own. Her father avoided her, and her mother didn't understand her reasoning—that they were supposed to stay together through the good and the bad. Besides, from her vantage point, how bad was their life, really? Her mother claimed her father never listened to her, and when she called her father, he said her mother didn't support him. Weren't those both typical problems they could talk through?

The most upsetting aspect was they'd gone to church all her life, and now they rarely went. Her mother said they'd attended church for the children, and her dad said he was too busy. This confused her. Their reasoning sounded silly and selfish—the total opposite of how they'd been during her childhood.

What really baffled her was how lightly they seemed to take the split. Her mother told her it had nothing to do with her. They'd both moved on with their lives, and they said they couldn't understand why she refused to do the same.

Her throat constricted, and a knot formed in her stomach as she thought about it. Her parents were no different from anyone else, it seemed.

When she couldn't eat another bite, she scraped the contents of her plate into the trash and stuck the plate in the dishwasher. Then she opened her purse and pulled out Jeremy's note. If she called him, she might have to answer questions. However, if she didn't call him, he might stop by unannounced and ask questions anyway.

She finally sucked in a breath, grabbed the phone, punched in his number, and exhaled. Maybe he wouldn't be able to talk. She could only hope. . . .

"Jeremy?" she said as soon as he answered.

"I was afraid you wouldn't call."

"What did you need?" she asked.

"I don't want to discuss it on the phone. When can we get together?"

"I don't know, Jeremy."

"Sorry if I'm annoying you, but I need to explain some things, and I won't give up until we have another chance to talk."

Cindi decided it was time to give in. "I'll look at my schedule and let you know, okay?"

"Sounds good," he said. "I'll see you soon, okay? My mom wants me to help her with something, so I need to run."

"Okay, fine."

She needed to go to bed early because they were booked full the next day. However, it took what seemed like hours to fall asleep. She was glad when daylight finally came so she could get busy and not have her head filled with so many thoughts of Jeremy.

Their first appointment arrived right on time, with Jeremy right behind them. The young bride and her mother were deep in discussion as they entered. Jeremy stepped off to the side so they could assist their customers.

"I've changed my mind," the bride said. "I hope you haven't started altering my dress yet." She'd chosen one of the samples on sale, and it needed to be taken in a few inches at the waist.

Elizabeth shook her head. "I was going to do yours next, so you're okay."

Cindi pulled out the checkbook. "I'll write you a check for your refund. Good thing you're backing out now rather than after the wedding."

The bride's mother laughed. "Oh, that's not what she meant. She's still getting married, but she decided to go with the other dress."

Cindi felt the heat rise to her cheeks. "I'm so sorry I assumed—"

The woman laughed again and waved her hand. "I certainly understand. Don't worry about it." She turned toward her daughter. "Do you remember which dress you liked? I sure hope they still have it."

"We do," Elizabeth interjected. "In fact, it's right here." She crossed the room and lifted a dress from one of the racks. "Why don't I set you up in the second fitting room so I can pin it?"

The bride and her mother went into the room, and Elizabeth followed right behind them with her pincushion. Cindi stayed behind the counter, still embarrassed by her faux pas.

As soon as they were out of earshot, Jeremy joined her at the counter. "It was an honest mistake," he said. "Don't worry so much about it."

"I'm not worried," she snapped.

He grinned and winked. "*Sure* you're not."

Elizabeth ducked her head out of the room. "They want another opinion, Cindi. Would you mind taking a look?"

"Sure." Cindi darted into the room to help out, leaving Jeremy behind in the showroom. As soon as she saw the dress on the young woman, she gave a thumbs-up. "Gorgeous! I agree this one is much better."

Elizabeth circled the stand. "It doesn't need much alteration, either. In fact, she could actually get away with only one small tuck."

The mother-of-the-bride had wandered over by the door and was looking out into the showroom. She stepped back in, looked directly at Cindi, and said, "Do you think your husband would mind giving us a man's opinion?"

Cindi shot her a curious look. "Husband?"

"Yes, that young man you were talking to when we arrived. He is your husband, isn't he?"

"Uh, no, he's not my husband."

The woman shook her head and smiled apologetically. "I'm terribly sorry. I was just telling my daughter what a cute couple you were."

Cindi was rendered speechless, and she glanced over in time to catch Elizabeth silently snickering. Her voice caught in her throat, and she couldn't speak.

"He might not be your husband, but he seems like a nice young man. Does he work here with you?"

In unison, Elizabeth and Cindi said, "No!"

"Do you think he'd mind telling us what he thinks of my daughter's dress?"

Elizabeth told Cindi to stay right where she was while she went to ask Jeremy. Cindi was thankful for the reprieve. Facing him immediately after the woman's innocent but clearly misguided comment would have been next to impossible.

seven

"The dress is beautiful," Jeremy announced. "I'm sure the groom will consider himself a very fortunate man."

The mother-of-the-bride's chest swelled with pride. "I think so, too, but of course I would."

"Seriously, she looks great. I think you made an excellent decision." He glanced at Cindi, but to her surprise, he didn't look the slightest bit uncomfortable. "But I didn't see the other dress on her, so I don't have anything to compare this one to."

The woman's eyebrows shot up. "Would you like to see the other one on her so you can compare them?"

"Mo—om," the bride moaned. "I'm sure he has better things to do with his time than stand around a bridal shop with a bunch of strangers."

"Oh, I don't mind," he said. "In fact, I'd love to see the other dress." He turned to Cindi. "That is, if you have the time."

What could Cindi say now? He'd put her on the spot in front of a valued customer. "We're okay on time. Our next appointment isn't for another twenty minutes."

As Cindi ushered him away from the fitting room, the bride's mother said, "Just keep in mind the other dress will need many more alterations."

Once the fitting room door closed, he looked at Cindi with contrition. "Sorry if this is inconveniencing you."

"Oh, don't be ridiculous, Jeremy. This is what I do all day. It's not an inconvenience."

"Whoa. Looks like I might have pushed a hot button."

Before she had a chance to defend her reaction, the fitting room door opened and out stepped the bride. Jeremy tilted his head to one side and studied her for a few seconds; then he moved around to get a view from a different angle. "It looks very pretty, but I agree with you all. The other one is perfect. It accents all your best features, while this one calls too much attention from your face."

The bride's mother beamed. "You have a great eye. Have you thought about going into the bridal business?"

Cindi was instantly stunned speechless. Elizabeth started coughing. Jeremy chuckled. "Yes, I've thought about it."

"Oh, you ought to do it. You'd be very good. Not many men would be as comfortable as you in a roomful of women voicing their honest opinion."

Jeremy thanked her then took a step back. "Great chatting with you ladies, but I need to run." He headed for the door then stopped, turned, and faced Cindi. "I'll call you later."

The bride's mother didn't waste a moment before turning to Cindi. "Who is that man?"

"His name is Jeremy Hayden, and he's a businessman who is trying to establish himself here in Atlanta," Cindi replied, trying hard not to let on how she felt deep down.

"I'll definitely be watching for him. If he has a business I can use, I'll be one of his best customers."

After the bride and her mother left, Elizabeth turned to Cindi. "If he winds up owning a bridal shop, I sure hope she has more than one daughter."

Cindi laughed. "Yeah, me, too."

Elizabeth suddenly grew serious. "So has he completely backed off trying to buy this place?"

"Looks that way."

"That was a fast change of heart."

"Yeah, it was, wasn't it?"

Elizabeth shrugged. "I never saw him in action until today. He has finesse."

"It's all a ruse to get what he wants," Cindi reminded her. "Remember? He's always been good at going after the prize then losing interest."

❧

Jeremy left the shop with an odd feeling in the pit of his stomach. Giving his opinion to that bride actually made him feel good—much better than when he worked in the candy store he'd first purchased years ago on a whim. He'd been looking for something to do with his life after the army. He got what he thought would be a temporary job working behind the counter—until something better came along. Then when the owner got in some financial trouble and said he'd have to either sell the shop or close it, Jeremy impulsively made a lowball offer. To his surprise, it was accepted. Once he owned the place, he made a few changes, hired people who knew how to sell, and offered samples. Those few things brought great rewards. He bought the video store next door when the owner had to leave the country.

When Jeremy grew tired of the candy store, he offered a special seller-financing deal to his employees, who jumped at the chance to own their own business. He carried the business skills he'd learned there to the video store and his next business after that and made it a point to learn everything he could to be successful.

His parents had been surprised at his business acumen and called it instinct. However, Jeremy knew better. He worked hard, learned from his mistakes, and treated people fairly—from the employees and vendors to the customers.

He now had a better understanding of the allure of running a bridal shop besides the business aspect. What would Cindi say if he told her he'd reconsidered and wanted to run it himself? Would she believe him?

He'd have to talk to her later, when she wasn't staring back at him with a look of distrust. Elizabeth, on the other hand, had actually smiled at him—a major feat as far as he was concerned. He'd sensed a lack of connection when he'd first come back, most likely due to Elizabeth's deep devotion to her lifelong best friend. Ever since he could remember, those two had practically been joined at the hip. One could almost always finish the other's sentences. There were times in high school when he'd felt a little jealous of what they had.

Sure, he'd had friends, but the relationships were mostly built around sports. He played basketball, so he and his teammates picked up games off-season on weekends. But when it was over, they either headed out for food or went their separate ways. There was never anyone he could talk to about anything meaningful.

When Cindi had brought him to church, he felt like a misfit, so he found ways to avoid it. At the time, he figured his parents managed to get by without it, so what was the point? However, now he knew that without Christ, life didn't hold much meaning beyond the here and now, and where was the joy in that? Once something in this world was gone, it was over. With the Christian perspective he now had, he realized how valuable life was and what he had to look forward to in eternity.

When he first became a believer, he thought once he got out of the army he might give up all his worldly possessions and go into the ministry. However, the base chaplain explained that not all believers are called to do that.

"The Lord wants us to go out and spread the gospel through everyday life. Being in the service or taking on the role of a successful businessman gives you quite a few opportunities to be in places I'm not likely to be."

So he'd prayed about it and made the decision to finish out his army stint and focus on opportunities to share the Word. He loved the Lord now, and he understood what Cindi had believed since childhood.

When he got home that night, his parents told him they wanted to go back to the same church. He was ecstatic and let them know how much that meant to him.

After his mother left the room, his dad asked him to sit down. "I think this is the very thing we've needed for a long time, but I'm still worried I'll look stupid because a man my age should know more about the Bible."

Jeremy jumped up. "Stay right here, Dad! I've got another great book that'll help."

He went to his room, dug into his nightstand drawer, and pulled out a book he'd been given when he first started attending church. It explained a little more than the basics of Christianity, and that bit of knowledge armed him with confidence. What better person to give it to than his dad?

"What's this all about, son?" His dad turned the book over and studied the back flap.

"A friend in Savannah gave it to me, and it helped me with the very thing you're worried about."

His dad's eyes lit up. "Oh, okay. It has answers to some of my questions. Mind if I borrow it for a few days so your mother and I can look through it?"

"Keep it, Dad. After you and Mom read it, you can pass it on to someone else who needs it."

Jeremy felt closer to his father than he'd ever been in his life. Amazing what coming to the Lord had done for him.

On Sunday Jeremy and his parents got to church early so they could find a good seat. His mother said she didn't like sitting in the back, so they moved closer toward the middle. He tried to avoid any confrontation with Cindi, because he didn't want her to think he was there for anything besides worship.

His mother belted out the worship songs, while his dad was more reserved. That was okay, though, because he was there worshipping his Savior. Jeremy felt as if he might burst with joy.

After church he and his parents made it all the way out to the parking lot when he heard someone call his name. He turned around and spotted Elizabeth running toward them.

"Why didn't you tell us you were coming?" she asked.

"I didn't think I needed to," he replied. "Besides, I don't want to annoy Cindi any more than I already have."

He saw the corners of Elizabeth's lips start to curl into a smile, but she caught herself. "Well, I just wanted to welcome you."

"Thank you, Elizabeth," Jeremy said.

His mother stepped forward. "Why don't you, your husband, and Cindi stop over for dinner later?"

"Um. . ." Elizabeth nervously glanced over her shoulder. "I don't think so. Not today."

"Mom," Jeremy said softly.

"Okay, okay, I'm sorry I embarrassed you. I shouldn't do that to you."

"You didn't embarrass me," he said.

Elizabeth took a step back. "I really need to run."

Jeremy held up a finger to get her to wait and turned to his mom. "Why don't you two go ahead and get in the car? I want to talk to Elizabeth for a moment, okay?"

His mother looked nervously back and forth between Jeremy and Elizabeth. "You won't be long, will you?"

"No, of course not." After his parents were safely out of listening range, he turned back to Elizabeth. "I wanted to let you know I'd never do anything to hurt Cindi or her shop. All I wanted—"

"You don't have to explain anything to me. It's between you and Cindi."

He could tell she still didn't completely trust him. All she'd wanted to do was show good manners and welcome him and his parents. He pursed his lips then smiled. "I understand."

Elizabeth started walking away but quickly turned. "By the way, Cindi loves vanilla mocha drinks from that coffee shop down the street."

He chuckled. "Thanks for the tip."

Once he and his parents got in the car, his mother turned to him. "What was that all about?"

"Nothing. Just chitchat about business."

"I hope you're not still trying to buy that bridal shop from Cindi."

"Mom, please leave my business dealings to me. It's not open for discussion."

She lifted her hands in surrender. "Whatever you say, Jeremy. Who am I to understand what's going on between you and that girl? You've never let love get in the way of what you wanted before, so why should I expect it to start now?"

That comment bothered Jeremy more than he wanted to admit. He thought about it the rest of the afternoon, and it woke him up in the middle of the night. Maybe his mother was right. Perhaps he should take a step back and look at his life from a different angle. He lay there staring at the ceiling for a few minutes before he decided to stop worrying so much.

He shut his eyes and prayed for direction, only now he prayed specifically for what to do with Cindi. By now, he knew he loved her even more than he had as a high school kid. He finally fell asleep, only to be awakened by his alarm clock.

He thought about what his mother had said all the way to the shop, and he knew she was probably right. He stopped off at the coffee shop for a couple of vanilla mocha drinks then headed to Cindi's Bridal Boutique.

Elizabeth grinned when she saw him come through the door. "How nice of you!" she said a little too loudly, letting him know she wanted Cindi to hear. "Cindi!" she hollered. "Jeremy brought us something wonderful!"

Cindi came from the back looking puzzled. When she spotted the coffee shop logo cups, she gave him a quizzical look.

"A little birdie told me you liked vanilla mocha."

She lifted one eyebrow and shot a glance in Elizabeth's direction. "I wonder who that little birdie is." A softer look covered her face when she turned back to him. "I saw you in church with your parents yesterday. I think it's nice you're bringing your family to worship."

Jeremy sensed Cindi's shell was starting to crack. He knew once that happened, he had the ability to totally knock it away by really pouring on the charm. But that was his old self. Although he never meant any harm, he didn't want to do anything that remotely hinted of underhandedness. He wanted her to trust him without any of the smoke and mirrors he once relied on to get what he wanted from people.

❧

Cindi's first reaction when she'd seen Jeremy in church had been that he was more persistent than anyone she'd ever known, and she'd put up her defense for when he approached her. However, he hadn't bothered to come up to her or use the church in any way. In fact, he seemed to be hiding from her. Elizabeth talked to her and said that in spite of her earlier concerns, she now felt Jeremy had sincerely become a Christian.

She'd thought about it all Sunday afternoon and lay in bed thinking about it half the night. She prayed about her own judgment, and when she woke up, she felt a heavy weight lift. In fact, she actually looked forward to the next time she saw Jeremy.

The vanilla mocha drink was a bonus.

"Thanks for the coffee," she said as she reached for it. "I really need it this morning."

"I wish I liked coffee," he admitted. "It smells good, but I still don't like the taste."

"Just enjoy the aroma." She lifted the lid and moved the coffee cup in the front of him. "Wanna try a little?"

He leaned over and inhaled. "It doesn't smell as strong as hot coffee, but I have to admit, I'd be tempted to taste it if I didn't know what it was like."

"I remember how much you used to enjoy milk shakes and malts."

"Still do," he said as he patted his belly. "But I can't indulge as much as I used to."

Elizabeth backed away from them. "I have to finish a hem, so I'll leave the two of you alone."

Cindi felt a little awkward chatting with Jeremy like this, but it wasn't too bad. He did seem very nice, and after Elizabeth had that talk with her, she sensed Jeremy was relaxing and not being so pushy.

"So did your folks enjoy church?"

He nodded. "Yes, very much so. In fact, my dad has been asking quite a few questions. I gave him a book someone gave me when I first came to Christ."

"You really are a Christian now, aren't you?"

"Yes," he said with a nod. "I really am."

Joy filled her heart. "That's the best news ever."

❧

He stood and watched her for a moment until a customer entered. That gave him an excuse to edge toward the door.

After he said good-bye, he overheard her asking questions about the needs of the bride-to-be, and he was impressed with her subtle salesmanship. Cindi handled each customer as if she was the most important person in Cindi's life. It was obvious she truly loved what she did, and it was the perfect work for her. He went straight to the real estate office and asked for Fran.

While he waited, he flipped through some of the residential booklets and spotted a couple of houses that appealed to him. Fran came out ten minutes later.

"Hi, Jeremy. What can I help you with?" she said as she clasped her hands together. "I have an appointment in about an hour, but if you'd like to come back to my office, I can spare a few minutes."

He followed her through the maze of offices until they reached her tiny office with the window overlooking Peachtree Street. He sat down in the chair across from her desk.

"I'd like to start looking at other businesses," he said right off the bat.

"Are you still interested in the bridal shop?"

He paused then said, "Not at the moment. I need to see how things work out between the owner and me."

She leaned forward and leveled him with a concerned look. "I don't normally recommend potential buyers spend so much time talking to the sellers, but when I realized the two of you knew each other from a long time ago, I didn't say anything."

Jeremy nodded. "I'm beginning to think it might have been a huge mistake for me to keep going over there. She might be getting the wrong idea about my intentions. It's hard for me to forget how I used to be, but I know now that I need to leave my old, immature self behind. I don't think I really want to buy the shop anymore. All I want is to buy a good business, boost the earnings, then sell it for a big profit."

He saw Fran's glance dart to something behind him, so he quickly turned around. There stood Elizabeth looking down at him with a scowl on her face, and he fidgeted, wondering if he'd done something wrong.

eight

"Elizabeth," he said with a smile. "What are you doing here?"

She didn't smile back. "I just came to talk to my friend who works here. She said you were with Fran, so I wanted to stop by to say hi." Her eyes had narrowed, and she was still scowling.

"Are you okay?" he asked, hoping she'd let him know what was going on.

Instead, she shook her head. "I almost believed you."

Fran looked back and forth between Jeremy and Elizabeth, then stood. "I'll leave the two of you alone so you can talk."

Elizabeth shook her head. "That's not necessary. I've heard all I need to hear."

Jeremy stood up to leave. Something strange was happening here, and he didn't want to make it worse.

As she made her way to the door, Elizabeth turned to him. "Don't bother following me. I don't have anything else to say to you."

❧

Cindi had just taken out the last of the shipment and hung it to be steamed. When she heard the door, she turned and saw Elizabeth moving toward her with a mission.

"I was right about Jeremy Hayden."

"What?" Cindi said, confused. "What happened?"

Elizabeth was clearly out of breath. She stood there, her chest heaving as she tried to compose herself. Finally, she let out a deep breath and said, "Be careful!"

"You're not making a bit of sense, Elizabeth. Tell me what's going on."

Cindi guided Elizabeth toward the love seat and encouraged her to explain what had happened. Then she listened as Elizabeth told her about the encounter with Jeremy at Fran's office.

"You were right," she said. "He was still planning to buy and sell your shop."

"You've been saying that all along, so why are you so upset now?"

"He so much as admitted to Fran that you were getting the wrong idea about his intentions and all he wanted to do was turn a profit after boosting the earnings. He's playing games with you just to make a buck."

A sense of dread washed over Cindi. She'd just started letting down her guard with Jeremy.

Elizabeth looked up and shook her head. "He's super slick."

"Okay, so what now?" Cindi asked.

"Since he has a history of being too charming for a nice girl like you, I suggest you avoid him at all costs. He isn't any different now from when he dumped—" She stopped midsentence.

Cindi lifted her eyebrows. "That's virtually impossible."

"I'll tell him to get lost if you want me to," Elizabeth offered.

"No," Cindi said. "I don't want to react to anything he does. That'll make him think I'm weak. I can still talk to him."

"I don't want to see you get hurt again," Elizabeth said softly.

"I realize that," Cindi replied as she turned to her friend and smiled. "I'll be careful, but I don't want to turn my back on him, now that he's at least going to church."

Elizabeth paused then nodded. "You're right. Just remember you can count on me to run interference if needed."

Cindi belted out a laugh. "I've never doubted you'd do that

for me. Now let's get back to work. We have a crazy day ahead of us, and it looks like it might be that way for the remainder of the week."

Their next appointment involved a family—bride, mother-of-the-bride, aunt on her mother's side, very young aunt on the groom's side, her sister, the groom's sister, and a couple of very wiggly, giggly flower girls from both sides of the family. In spite of the extra time they required, this was one of Cindi's favorite scenarios. She loved the dynamics of the blended families, and she found the children delightful.

"Mommy, I want this dress!" one of the little girls shouted across the store. "Can I have this dress? It looks like a princess dress."

The other girl looked at it before turning to Cindi. "I'm a flower girl, and so is she." The sassiness in her voice was funny, but Cindi could tell this one was a handful.

"How fun!" Cindi said. She looked up at the bride-to-be. "I'll get Elizabeth to work with the flower girls, and then I'll help you all. Did you want them in long white dresses?"

The bride glanced at her mother, who nodded. "I'm pretty open."

Elizabeth grinned at the little girls. "Let's go try on a bunch of princess dresses, and we'll see what looks best, okay?"

"Oh, goody! We get to play dress up!"

Cindi asked the bride all the pertinent questions, such as what style wedding dress she wanted and what colors she wanted her bridesmaids to wear. Cindi sensed the bride was overwhelmed by all the choices, so she leaned toward the woman. "You don't have to make a decision today," she whispered.

The bride smiled at her and nodded. "Thanks."

All the pressure had been lifted, so the bride and her entourage finally enjoyed trying on dresses. The women chattered while the little girls squealed and giggled.

Cindi had to rescue a couple of the mannequins from the children, but she didn't mind. They were excited, and they brought such joy and fun energy to the room. She'd always enjoyed being around children.

"Here are some wedding gown brochures." Cindi handed them to the bride. When she saw that the other women looked left out, she handed them some brochures from the designer the bride seemed to prefer.

The groom's aunt looked startled for a split second, then straightened up. "Oh, thanks," she said as she took it.

Cindi gave the bride her card and told her to call back by the end of the day to schedule the second appointment. As the bridal party left, Cindi glanced at Elizabeth, who made a face and pointed to the corner of the room.

She looked in the direction Elizabeth pointed and saw Jeremy standing there, arms folded, looking amused. How long had he been watching?

Once the women were gone, he slowly ambled to the counter. "You did an amazing job once again, Cindi. I continue to be impressed."

"Give me a break," Elizabeth said.

Jeremy and Cindi both snapped around to face her. Cindi realized her friend was feeling protective of her, but she needed to hold back the sarcasm.

"Excuse me for a minute, Jeremy," Cindi said as she took Elizabeth by the arm and ushered her into the fitting room. Once she had her friend alone, she turned to her. "Let me handle him, okay?"

"It annoys me that he thinks he can wear you down," Elizabeth argued.

Cindi loved that about Elizabeth, but she could take care of herself. "I know, but remember he can't wear me down unless I let him." She looked around the room at some of the mess left behind by the last group. "Why don't you take care of reboxing those shoes, and I'll join you to get this place straightened up after I get rid of Jeremy?"

"Be strong," Elizabeth said as Cindi left the room.

"What was that all about?" Jeremy asked.

Cindi crossed her arms and looked him in the eye. This was no time for mincing words. "She's trying to protect me."

"From what?"

"You."

The expression on his face went from confused to understanding. "I thought she'd finally warmed up to me, but she hasn't, has she?"

"Not at all."

"That's not good." He looked around the room while Cindi continued staring at him. He looked very uncomfortable. Almost a minute later, he finally settled his gaze on her. "Why don't we—the two of us—get together and talk?"

"We can talk now," Cindi said as she glanced at her watch. "I don't have another appointment for a while."

The phone rang, so she excused herself to answer it since Elizabeth was still in the fitting room. She answered some questions then turned back to Jeremy.

He tilted his head forward. "I think we need to go somewhere else without the distractions. How about tonight after work. Got plans for tonight?"

"Uh. . ." She didn't have plans, and she didn't want to lie, but the very thought of going somewhere alone with him worried her. His mere presence sent her senses into a spin.

"Or another night this week. I don't want to put you on the spot. I just want to let you know what's going on with me and what I've decided. And I think there are a few other things we need to discuss."

Cindi took a step back and thought it over while he silently waited. It was unnerving having him standing there so close scrutinizing her every move. If going somewhere to talk meant removing the distraction of him always popping in like this, she figured she needed to agree.

"Okay, tonight will be just fine. Want to meet somewhere?"

A smile played on his lips. "How about Chastain Park?"

Suddenly she felt herself go numb. Chastain Park was where they used to go when they were teenagers. And it was where he first kissed her.

"How about someplace else?" she asked.

He narrowed his gaze. "What's wrong with Chastain Park?"

"Nothing." She didn't want to let on how she'd clung to certain memories, so she fidgeted behind the counter, pretending to look for something. "We can meet at Chastain Park if it's so important to you."

"How about we meet at the playground by the pavilion?"

She swallowed deeply. That was the exact spot where he first kissed her. Without looking him in the eye, she said, "Okay, we can meet there, but not for long."

"I understand. You're a busy woman."

She couldn't tell if he was serious or if he was being sarcastic. "I really need to get back to work, Jeremy. Elizabeth is closing up tonight, so I can leave around five thirty."

"See you at six, then," he said. "Oh, and don't make plans for dinner. There's a wonderful place I'd like to take you."

Before she had a chance to tell him she wasn't available for dinner, he left. Elizabeth came out of the fitting room.

"Well?" she asked.

❧

Jeremy was fully aware he had one shot at showing Cindi his integrity after the way Elizabeth had acted. Something new had happened, and he aimed to find out what it was. Also, it was time to let Cindi know what happened many years ago, but he wasn't sure if she wanted to hear it.

He pulled out his phone and punched in his mother's work number. She answered immediately.

"Mom, do you mind if I bring a guest home for dinner?"

"Of course I don't mind. I'm cooking stew in the Crock-Pot, though. It's nothing special."

"I think that's pretty special. I'll stop somewhere and get bread and dessert. Anything else you need?"

"No." There were a few seconds of silence before she asked, "Is it Cindi?"

"Yes."

"That's good. I like her."

"Yes, I know."

"Maybe one of these days you'll feel like you can trust me enough to let me in on the details of what happened between you two."

He didn't feel like explaining anything, so he mumbled a few words then told her he had to run. After he flipped his phone shut, he went back to Fran's office. She wasn't in, so he left a message that he'd be in touch the next day.

Jeremy went to his parents' condo and ran the vacuum. His mother worked hard all day, and he didn't want her to feel as if she had to do additional work when she got home. As things changed, he wanted to adapt and make the lives of his loved ones easier. He hadn't always been that way, and he felt the need to make up for those times.

After the place was clean, he ran out for bread, dessert, and drinks. Then he got ready for his date. . . . *No, better not think about it that way.* For his *meeting* with Cindi.

❧

Cindi's nerves were on edge when she arrived at Chastain Park. She parked her car and headed straight to their meeting spot. Not much appeared to have changed since she'd last been here. Chastain Park was huge, and she'd been to a couple of concerts at the amphitheater, but this was the first time she'd been back to this spot. *Their* spot.

She was a few minutes early, so she hoped she'd get there first. However, once she got closer, she saw Jeremy standing there waiting—a flower in his hand. Her heart fluttered.

nine

"I remembered how much you like white roses," he said as he extended the flower.

She hesitated before reaching out to take it. "Thank you," she said softly.

"How was work since I last saw you? Did you have a calm afternoon?"

Cindi chuckled. "It's all relative. It was calmer than what you saw, but there were a few tense moments when a bride changed her mind about a dress after it was altered."

"That's not good."

"We've had this sort of thing happen before, and you're right—it's not a good thing. Once a dress has been altered, most vendors won't let us send it back, so we're stuck."

His forehead crinkled. "So you're stuck with the dress?"

"Not this time, fortunately. She told us what she wanted different, and we managed to reconfigure the dress to her liking."

"It's good you can do that," he said.

Again, Cindi laughed. "It's good Elizabeth can do that. Not a day goes by that I'm not thankful for her fabulous seamstress skills. She can make almost any alteration and customize dresses so brides feel they're having gowns made especially for them."

Cindi wondered when they'd cut the small talk and get to whatever he wanted to discuss with her. Her feelings were mixed. In a way, she wanted to get whatever it was over with, but she didn't feel like confronting anything distasteful.

She looked up at him in time to see a familiar gaze—identical to the one they'd shared right before he told her he loved her.

"It's a nice evening, isn't it?" He reached out and touched her cheek with the back of his hand.

"Yes, it's a very nice evening," she said as she looked at the ground. Each time she looked at him in this setting, old memories flashed through her mind.

ટ•

Jeremy felt Cindi might be warming up to him, but as quickly as she looked up at him, she seemed nervous. "What are you thinking, Cindi?"

Without missing a beat, she asked, "Why did you want me to meet you here?"

"There are some things I needed to explain."

Cindi took a step back and folded her arms. "Okay, so start explaining."

He saw the distrust on her face. "Do you remember what I told you the first time we were here?"

She wanted to deny she remembered anything, but she couldn't. With a slight nod, she sniffled.

"I meant it then, and I mean it now."

"How can you say that, Jeremy, after what you did to me later?"

He tightened his jaw. This was one of the most difficult things he'd ever done in his life—but still not as hard as letting her go.

"When I told you I didn't love you anymore, I was lying. I just wanted you to be free to pursue your dreams."

"So you said. That's ridiculous."

"Is it?" he asked as he lowered his head and held her gaze.

"It makes no sense. We were supposedly in love. Everything was going just fine."

"For you, maybe. You had colleges begging you to attend."

She snickered. "Not really begging me. I just got accepted to a few that I applied to."

"That's what I'm talking about," he said. "I had nothing. No college. No hopes for the future. No dreams."

"Everyone has hopes and dreams."

"Trust me when I tell you this, Cindi. I had no idea what I'd do the day after graduation, let alone for the rest of my life. I figured if I didn't let you go, I'd be holding you back from a prosperous life."

"You've been at least as prosperous as I have," she replied.

"Maybe. But I didn't know it would turn out this way back then."

She shrugged. "Okay, so now what?"

"I'm not sure. But I'd like to find out if we can bring back something we once had."

She tilted her head and looked at him before her lips turned up at the corners into a smile. "Let me think about it, okay?"

"Fair enough," he agreed. "Want to go for a walk?"

She lifted one shoulder then let it drop as she offered a slight grin. "Sure, why not?"

They meandered around a small area of the park and talked about anything that came to mind. She was a great conversationalist, something he remembered about her from high school. In fact, it was one of the many things he'd loved about her.

"So tell me more about how you came to faith," she said.

He told her all about his commanding officer's gentle witness and how he'd been willing to answer even the most basic of questions. She nodded and interjected a few comments, which let him know she was really listening. He could tell when she softened toward him because she looked at him with more trust than he'd seen since they were teenagers.

"That's a really nice story," she said after he told her about his Christian journey. "How about your parents? When did they start going to church?"

"Just recently. In fact, your church is the first one they've gone to since I can remember."

"You're kidding." She looked sincerely surprised. "They seem comfortable."

"Yeah, I noticed that, too." He stopped walking and reached out to turn her toward him. "Cindi. . ."

A brief look of fear came over her face as she took a step back, so he didn't finish his sentence. He'd been about to tell her he was comfortable, too—both in church and when he was with her. But based on the look she gave him, now wasn't the time.

Instead, he chose a different topic. "Are you hungry?"

A quick giggle escaped her lips. "Hungry?" She visibly relaxed, and her fearful look faded. "You've always thought about food."

"Yeah, well, maybe so, but food's important. I'd like to take you someplace special."

"I don't know," she said. "I really don't feel like eating out tonight."

"This is sort of like not eating out."

"You're talking in riddles, Jeremy. Where do you want to take me?"

"My folks'."

"Um, I don't think that's such a good idea." She shifted her weight from one foot to the other as she appeared to grow uncomfortable again.

"I thought you liked my parents. My mom adores you."

Cindi smiled as she looked back at him. "I think your parents are very nice people. What I don't understand, though, is why you want to take me to their place."

He shrugged. "I thought it would be a nice thing for all of us."

"What have your parents been up to—besides going to church?"

Jeremy could hear the caring tone of her voice. Cindi had never looked down on him or his family, while other kids in school had made him feel bad because he wasn't as well off as most of them. Cindi treated him and his parents as if she didn't see any difference at all.

"They're doing a lot better, now that they're both working. They sold our old house and bought a nice condo a few years ago."

Cindi offered a sincere smile. "That's great. Your parents are good people."

"Then come have dinner with us. I called my mom and told her I was inviting you, and she was delighted."

"I *could* get mad about that," Cindi said with a throaty chuckle, "but I choose to be flattered instead." She paused for a moment before adding, "Okay, I'll go. But I want to bring something."

"You don't have to. I got bread and dessert to go with the meal she's been cooking in the Crock-Pot all day."

"I'm not going empty-handed."

"Fine. We can stop at the grocery store on the way. Why don't you leave your car here, and I can bring you back?"

She bought a basket of fruit to leave with them. "I remember your mother always put an apple in your lunch every day."

He laughed. "Yeah, she believed that old saying about an apple a day and the doctor."

"I believe that, too." Then she grew quiet as he took the last turn onto his parents' street.

Instinctively, he reached over and placed his hand on hers. She looked at him in surprise, but she didn't pull her hand out of his. It felt so right, he didn't ever want to move. Finally, he reluctantly withdrew his hand to maneuver his car into the driveway.

"Ready?" he asked.

She offered a quick nod then opened the door and got out. He ran around and escorted her to the open front door where his mother stood waiting.

"Hi, Mrs. Hayden," Cindi said. "It's really nice to see you again."

His mother opened her arms and pulled Cindi in for a long embrace. "You've become quite a beautiful young woman. I'm glad my son got in touch with you so I could see for myself."

"I brought this for you." Cindi handed his mother the fruit basket.

Jeremy ushered them all inside as his mother protested that she wasn't expecting a gift, but Cindi told her she was happy to bring it. Warmth flooded him from his head to his toes as he realized how much it meant to him to have his two favorite women together.

"So this is the girl you should have married."

All heads turned toward the booming voice at the foot of the stairs. "Now, James, you shouldn't embarrass them. Cindi's our guest for dinner."

"I know," he continued, "it's just that—"

"Dad." Jeremy was angry with his father, but he forced himself to keep his voice low and his temper cool. He didn't want to make Cindi squirm any more than she was now.

His father darted a glance over at Cindi then looked back at him. "Sorry, son, I guess that was uncalled for." He looked back at Cindi. "I like your church. The people seem pretty nice, and that preacher is a mighty interesting fella, even if he is young enough to be my son."

"Yes," Cindi said as she visibly relaxed. Jeremy was relieved she could recover so quickly. "He's good at holding our interest without losing the message we all need to hear."

"I think we just might keep going back." He rubbed his neck. "What's for dinner, Donna? I had a rough day, and I'm starving."

&

Cindi remembered how kind, spontaneous, and full of life Jeremy's parents were, and they hadn't changed a bit. Every occasion in their home was centered around food, something she could tell hadn't changed. No wonder Jeremy was always thinking about his next meal. His mother had always been very gracious and sweet, while his father was loud but deep down was a softy. They weren't as well off as most of the people in the area, but they had heart.

And they were still together, unlike her own parents.

After dinner, Cindi joined Jeremy's mother in the kitchen. "Go sit out there with the guys," the older woman said.

"What guys?" Jeremy asked as he rolled up his sleeves. "You mean Dad?" He took the stack of plates from his mother. "Why don't both of you go in there while I take care of the kitchen?"

"But it's a mess," his mother argued.

He looked around. "It's not that bad. Now shoo."

With a giggle, Mrs. Hayden took Cindi by the hand and led her to the living room where Mr. Hayden sat staring at the TV with the remote control in his lap. Without even glancing up, he bellowed, "Tell me all about college."

Cindi felt awkward and didn't know what to say, so she was grateful when Mrs. Hayden piped up, "She's been out of college for a long time, James." She glanced at Cindi. "What has it been—something like five years now?"

"Almost seven," Cindi corrected her.

Mrs. Hayden grinned as she turned back to her husband. "She's a businesswoman now."

"Okay," he said, shaking his head and giving them a silly look. "So tell me about business. I'm tired of talking about stuff that doesn't matter, but the wife gets mad when I don't behave at the table."

Cindi opened her mouth to answer, but again, Mrs. Hayden spoke for her. "She owns a bridal shop. You know that, James. I bet business is always good at that kind of place. Girls are always getting married."

"So what would you know about a bridal shop?" he asked Cindi. "You ever get married?"

"Um. . .no, sir," Cindi replied. Now she was more uncomfortable than ever. "I sort of learned the business as I went. I worked for a couple of years in retail after college and learned a little about working with customers. I lived with my parents, then got a roommate after college to save money." She didn't tell him about the humongous bank loans her parents cosigned for. She was thankful she'd been able to pay them off quickly.

"Well, I guess that's okay. So what all do you do at your bridal shop?"

Mrs. Hayden winked at her before turning to her husband. "She sells bridal gowns and bridesmaid dresses, silly."

"I think that's great. How much is a bridal gown, anyway?"

Cindi knew he was just making conversation, but the questions were starting to sound rude. She gave Mrs. Hayden a look for help. To her relief, the woman came to her rescue.

"That's not something you need to know, James. It's part of the bridal mystique."

He made a grumbling noise. "That just means they're way too expensive. Otherwise, you'd tell me. If brides had a lick of sense, they'd rent their dresses just like the guys do their tuxes."

Cindi could have told him there actually were bridal gown

rental shops, but she didn't want to get into all the reasons she wouldn't recommend them. Instead, she focused her attention on Mrs. Hayden.

"Dinner was delicious. I didn't know what to expect when Jeremy told me he wanted to take me someplace special."

Tears instantly formed in Mrs. Hayden's eyes. "He said that? What a sweet thing to say."

Jeremy appeared at the door wiping his hands on a dish towel. "Let me know when you're ready to go, and I'll take you back to your car."

Cindi stood. "Since we all have to work tomorrow, I'd better head out now. It was very nice seeing both of y'all again. Stop by the shop sometime."

Mrs. Hayden's eyes lit up, and she nodded. "I'd love to!"

Mr. Hayden grumbled, but then he stood and took her hand. "You're a good girl, Cindi. I'm glad you came over tonight."

On the way back to the park, Jeremy slipped a CD in the car stereo, and the strains of contemporary Christian music filled the air. Neither of them said anything until they were almost at the Chastain Park parking lot. Cindi was the first to talk.

"Thanks for bringing me to your parents' house. It was really nice."

"They love you, ya know. My mother was upset when we. . ." He cleared his throat then shrugged. "Anyway, maybe the two of you can chat after church sometime."

"I'd like that." After he stopped beside her car, she opened the door, got out, leaned over, and said, "If you want to come by the shop and see me sometime, well, maybe. . ."

His face lit up. "You can count on it."

That night she thought about everything that had happened and all Jeremy had said. Could it be possible she was wrong about him? What he'd done made sense in a childish sort of way—and since they were both children when it happened, she could understand. Jeremy seemed sincere in his faith, so that obviously put a different light on things. However, would she ever be able to forgive him for leaving her so brokenhearted?

The next morning when she got to the shop, Elizabeth was in the sewing room deeply immersed in alterations. She glanced up and waved. "How was last night?"

Cindi saw she wasn't smiling. "It was fun. I met Jeremy, and he took me to dinner at his parents' house."

"Oh my. He's pulling out all the stops, isn't he?"

"I've always liked his parents—especially his mom."

"So," Elizabeth said as she lowered the foot behind the sewing machine needle and flipped off the light switch, "what lines did he feed you to try to get you to sell him the shop?"

"No lines. We didn't talk about him buying the shop."

"I'm sure he's just waiting for the right time."

"Maybe, maybe not."

"Please, please don't fall for his charm again. You were so hurt before, and I'd hate for it to happen again."

Cindi nodded. "I appreciate your concern more than you know. I just see things differently now, so I'm fine. Even if he's got a hidden agenda, I can handle it."

There was nothing Elizabeth could say to that. She hung up the dress she'd been working on and joined Cindi at the desk. By the time the first appointment walked in, they were a cohesive team.

Jeremy showed up at noon. "Want some lunch?" he asked. He'd obviously inherited his mother's penchant for feeding people.

"Not today," Cindi replied. "I brought a sandwich I'll have to eat on the run. Are you trying to make me fat?"

"You look great, Cindi."

She felt her cheeks heat up. "Thank you."

"Maybe tomorrow?"

"Maybe." The phone rang, so she answered it.

He chatted with Elizabeth while she talked to the caller. Elizabeth still didn't believe him, and Cindi appreciated the fact that she was making an effort for her sake. After Cindi hung up, he said good-bye then left.

"I can say one thing for him," Elizabeth said once he was gone. "He's persistent."

"Which is probably why he's been so successful in business."

Jeremy stopped by a few more times that week. Cindi eventually gave in and went out with him. Elizabeth finally quit commenting, which was almost as bad as the interrogation. Cindi knew her friend still didn't trust him, but she was holding everything inside.

On Thursday morning Jeremy didn't show up. "This seems strange," Elizabeth said. "We never know when he's coming, so it's like we're always expecting him."

"I've found if I don't expect anything, I'm never disappointed," Cindi replied.

By the end of the day, Cindi was exhausted. Fran arrived just as they were about to leave. "Oh, good," she said. "You're still here. I just got a call from someone who's interested in taking a look at the shop."

Cindi's heart fell. "That's good." She was too tired to hide her remorse.

Fran frowned. "You do still want to sell, don't you?"

"Yes, of course. It's just been a long day, and I'm tired."

"If it's okay with you, then, I'll bring them by tomorrow around noon."

"Them?" Cindi paused.

"Yes, the prospects are a couple of newlyweds who think

this will be the perfect way to work together."

Elizabeth laughed. "Fancy that. A married couple who want to be together."

Cindi didn't miss the sarcasm. "Noon is fine."

"See you then," Fran said as she curiously glanced back and forth between Cindi and Elizabeth.

Once she was gone, Cindi stood and stared at the door of her shop. Elizabeth reached out and gently touched her shoulder.

"Having second thoughts about selling?"

"Sort of." Cindi stuck the key in the lock, turned it, and spun around to face Elizabeth. "But I'm sure that's normal. Now let's go home and get some rest. We have to impress some prospective buyers tomorrow."

The next morning, Cindi got to the shop before Elizabeth arrived. She changed a couple of the mannequins and rearranged the accessories case to give it a fresher look. Then she stepped back and admired her work. She'd miss many things about the business once she sold it, and this was one of them. It truly made her happy to help bring out a woman's pure beauty on her wedding day. Times like this made her stop and think—maybe she shouldn't sell. She still loved running her shop.

When the door opened, she expected it to be Elizabeth, but it wasn't. It was her mother.

"Mom, hi! What are you doing here?"

Her mother looked around and then turned to her. "The place looks really nice, Cindi. I just stopped by to see if you had plans for later. We need to talk." She gulped and added, "It's very important."

Cindi checked the appointment book to make sure she could leave early before replying, "I think Elizabeth will probably be able to stay until closing, and our last scheduled appointment is at three. I think I can be out of here by four."

Her mother's lips twitched as she nodded. "That'll be great. Have you spoken to your father lately?"

Slowly shaking her head, Cindi replied, "Not in several weeks. Why?"

"I'll tell you later."

Elizabeth walked in and gave Cindi's mother a hug. "Come by and see us more often, Reba," Elizabeth said.

"I just might do that. And if you're ever looking for someone to work part-time, I'm interested."

"What?" Cindi said.

"Look, Cindi, I've got to run. I'll see you this afternoon. I'll run by your place. . .four thirty?"

"Sounds good," Cindi said.

Once she was gone, Elizabeth tilted her head. "What was that all about?"

"I have no idea. I'll find out at four thirty if you can hang out here and close the shop."

"Yes, of course." Elizabeth opened the door to the sewing room then turned to face Cindi. "Looks like it'll be an eventful day for you."

"Certainly seems that way."

"Maybe this couple will be exactly what this shop needs," Elizabeth said with slow deliberation.

An odd sensation of internal free-falling came over Cindi. She turned away so Elizabeth wouldn't see her expression.

ten

Jeremy hesitated before heading toward Cindi's shop. She'd encouraged him to stop by to see her, something he'd been doing all along. However, he sensed a turning point in their relationship, and he wasn't sure if it was too soon.

And then there was Elizabeth. Cindi had warmed toward him, but it was painfully obvious Elizabeth didn't like him. He couldn't blame her, though—if someone had hurt one of his friends, he would have been just as protective. Perhaps a complete breakup hadn't been the right move, but he was just a kid, and that was all he knew to do at the time. He decided he'd given her enough time to work through things and it was time to talk to her about whatever issues she still had with him.

For nights he'd stared at the ceiling, unable to sleep, wondering what he'd been thinking. He couldn't erase Cindi from his mind—from the happy moments with her glowing smile to the look of despair when he'd told her he wanted his class ring back. It had taken every ounce of self-restraint to hold himself back when she refused to look at him again.

The army had been good for him. Not only did it provide him with a modest living, but he learned how to be a man. Fortunately for him, his commanding officer saw his need for Christ, which proved nothing was impossible for the Lord.

His candy store job was obviously not a career position, but the Lord had allowed him to be at the right place when the opportunity to make something of himself had come open. After buying it, he learned how to run a business the hard way. When he was twenty-six, he was listed as one of the

If the Dress Fits 115

youngest businessmen to watch in the state of Georgia. And now at twenty-nine, he was ready to settle down and stop trying to prove himself.

He was good at what he did and he enjoyed it, but traveling all over Georgia was wearing on him. It was time to go home to Atlanta and settle down. He'd now sold all of his businesses, with the exception of a men's shop in Savannah and a tire store in Macon.

An overwhelming urge to see Cindi again gave him the strength to head to her boutique. He'd have to be patient with Elizabeth and prove he'd changed.

As he pulled up in front of the bridal boutique, he saw Elizabeth by the window looking out. She looked his way then disappeared. His heart hammered as he thought about how he still felt toward Cindi.

"Hey, Elizabeth," he said as he entered the store.

"Hi." She forced a smile then went back to her paperwork.

"Is Cindi here yet?"

She lifted an eyebrow. "Not yet. Is there anything I can help you with?"

At least she was talking to him, but she didn't bother trying to hide her feelings. He decided to try to make small talk for a few minutes—partly to get a feel for how to win over the best friend of the woman he loved, but mostly to kill time until Cindi arrived. "How long have you been working with Cindi?"

She sighed. "Practically all my life."

"You make a great team."

"So we've been told."

Okay, so this wasn't going well at all. He racked his brain to try to think of another subject. "By the way," he began, "I've been thinking about that day in Fran's office."

Elizabeth turned to him, snorted, and shook her head. "Yeah, I think about that day myself."

"I'm not sure what happened—"

He was cut off when he heard a door close from the back of the store; then Cindi appeared. "Hey, you two." She glanced over at Elizabeth. "Any calls from the Hansen-Showers bridal party?"

"Not yet." Elizabeth's voice was still clipped.

Cindi gave her a puzzled look then turned to Jeremy with a smile. "We used to have a wedding season, but things are changing. There's almost an equal balance of weddings year-round these days."

Jeremy could take a hint. She was busy, but she didn't want to tell him to get lost. "I just wanted to stop by on my way to Fran's. She's supposed to line up some other businesses for me to look at."

He couldn't help but notice her quick gasp and odd expression. She recovered quickly and smiled. "I hope all goes well. I really need to get to work, though. See you later?"

"Sure." He lifted a hand in a wave and left the shop. The silence that fell behind him made him wonder what the women were thinking.

❧

"He must want this shop pretty badly to keep coming by like this," Elizabeth said as they stood in front of the open refrigerator staring at all the food.

Cindi sighed. "I'm not so sure I want to sell now, but if I do, I'm thinking he might be okay."

"How about that other couple Fran's supposed to bring by at noon?"

"I don't know them. I know Jeremy."

"I thought y'all decided to move on," Elizabeth argued. "He agreed to look for something else, and you're not selling to someone who won't be here to run it. How can you do that?"

With a shrug, Cindi replied, "No one else has made an offer. Besides, Jeremy just might have changed."

"Don't tell him that yet, okay?" Elizabeth pleaded. "I don't want to take any chances."

Cindi thought about how she had Elizabeth to think about as well as herself, so she shook her head no. "You're right. I'm not really in that big of a hurry anymore. I'll give it a little more time. Who knows? I might just keep it a little longer."

Fran brought the young prospects by the shop at the precise moment a difficult bride went on a tirade about none of the dresses fitting. The expression on the wife's face was priceless. Cindi wasn't surprised when the couple politely said they'd talk about it and have Fran get back with her.

"Looks like no sale," Elizabeth whispered.

"And that's probably a good thing," Cindi agreed. "If something that minor turns her off, she has no business owning a bridal shop."

"So true."

The next couple of hours were much calmer. Then a few minutes after three o'clock, Christina, one of the brides who'd gotten married a couple of months earlier, came in with her wedding photo proofs. "I wanted you to see how pretty all the girls looked," she said, "and Jonathan loved my gown. He said it was the prettiest wedding dress he'd ever seen."

"He would have said that no matter what you wore," Cindi said as she studied the pictures. "But you do look beautiful."

"Thanks to you two, I didn't have to worry about any of the dresses," Christina said. "I've heard some horror stories from my friends who got their dresses elsewhere."

"So how's your marriage?"

Christina sighed as a dreamy expression crossed her face. "The best."

After Christina left, Cindi saw Elizabeth staring at her. "Okay, I know what you're thinking. This is more proof that I need to keep the shop."

"You said it—I didn't," Elizabeth said. Her expression changed and became contemplative. "I wonder what's up with your mother."

Cindi grimaced. "I wish I knew. I'm worried about her."

"I've been praying for your parents. . .and you. I know how difficult this must be."

"Yeah, when your parents spring that kind of news on you, it's pretty jolting."

"Why don't you go on home now? I can take care of the shop from now on."

Cindi grabbed her keys and purse and headed home, where she immediately put on a fresh pot of coffee. By the time her mother arrived, the coffee was done.

"Who gave you the rose?" her mother asked as she leaned over and sniffed the single bloom in the vase in the middle of the kitchen table.

"Jeremy."

Her mom froze, eyes wide. Finally, she raised her eyebrows and said, "Jeremy? As in Jeremy Hayden?"

"The one and only."

"I heard he was in town. When did you see him?"

Cindi touched a finger on one hand and said, "Yesterday"; then she touched the next finger. "And the day before yesterday, and the day before that."

"So what's going on between you two?" Her mother poured herself a cup of coffee then sat down at the kitchen table. "I heard he was looking to buy a business and a house."

"For such a big city, word sure does travel fast," Cindi said.

"Well, it helps to know the Realtor's sister."

"I'll tell you all about it, but not until you let me know what's going on with you."

Her mother inhaled and then slowly blew out her breath. She shut her eyes for a couple of seconds the way she always did when she needed to gather her thoughts. "Your father and I have agreed to go to counseling. We're taking things slowly, but we'd like to try working on our problems."

Cindi's mood lifted instantly. "Really? That's wonderful news. When did you decide to do that?"

"A couple of weeks ago he stopped by to pick up a few things. I'd just baked a casserole, and since he hadn't eaten supper yet, I. . .well, I asked him to join me. You know how much I hate to eat alone."

"Yes," Cindi said as she leaned toward her mother. "So he ate dinner with you?"

Her mother nodded and smiled. "We had the best time, too. I'd forgotten what a great conversationalist he is."

Cindi shook her head. "What do you think happened?"

"I'm not sure, but the counselor I called said it was fairly common for couples to split up once the children are gone."

"And Daddy agreed to go to counseling?" Amazing.

"Yes, that's the best part. He said he'd been thinking about working things out, but he didn't know how to bring it up, and he was glad I took the first step." She fidgeted for a few seconds then looked at Cindi. "You know how your father's pride is."

"Yes, I remember that."

"I'm feeling pretty good about things. I hope you're happy."

Cindi let out a sigh of joy. "You couldn't have brought better news that would have made me any happier."

"Please pray for us, honey. I never stopped loving your father, and I want this to work out."

"Trust me, Mom, I'll pray night and day. I want it to work out as much as you do."

"Now tell me what's going on with your shop."

Cindi explained how she felt and why she was still selling. The whole time she talked, her mother never interjected a word until Cindi finally said, "What are you thinking?"

"I think you're making a huge mistake. You've always dreamed of running a bridal shop, and you're living your dream. How many other people can say that?"

"You of all people should understand why I don't want to perpetuate a myth—a fantasy that marriage is so wonderful."

"To be honest with you," her mother said softly, "it's as wonderful as a couple makes it. If two people keep their focus on the Lord and their family, they can work through almost anything. Being married to your father was almost like living my own fairy tale until one day everything seemed out of place."

"I still don't understand why you split up."

"Ya know, I'm not sure, either, but maybe we needed a little time apart to realize how good we had it together. The Lord let us separate, but don't forget we didn't divorce."

After her mother left, Cindi cleared the dishes and thought about how quickly things could change. She was relieved her parents seemed to be heading in the right direction.

The next day Cindi told Elizabeth about her parents' efforts to reconcile. "I feel so much better now," she admitted.

"Do you feel good enough to keep this place?"

"Maybe."

The conversation ended quickly when a bride came in frazzled and in tears because another bridal shop had messed up her order. "I have to have something by the week after next. Is that even possible?"

Cindi and Elizabeth exchanged a glance before they turned to her, nodding. "Yes, as long as you keep an open mind," Elizabeth said. "We can take one of our sample dresses and customize it for you."

By the time she left, the bride was shedding a different kind of tears—those of joy over the fact that she liked the dress Elizabeth was customizing even more than the one she'd originally found. "I'll tell all my friends about this place," she said. "You two are the very best!"

"That does it," Cindi said. "I think I'll withdraw my listing. I can't imagine letting someone suffer like that poor girl obviously was."

"Attagirl." Elizabeth grinned and nodded. "Back in the saddle and stronger than ever."

The rest of the day went smoothly. Cindi was so happy about her decision, she felt as if she were walking on clouds. Elizabeth kept looking at her and giving her the thumbs-up gesture.

On Sunday Cindi arrived at church early and watched for Jeremy. When she didn't see him by the time the first song began, she focused all her attention on the service. During private prayer time, she thanked the Lord again for her parents' reconciliation and asked for guidance with Jeremy. Her attraction had only grown stronger, yet she wasn't sure what to do.

After the closing benediction, Cindi turned toward the exit. That was when she spotted Jeremy, his mother, his dad, and. . .his brother, Jacob? She hadn't seen Jacob since high school when he'd come home to visit his parents. Jacob was several years older than them. He'd gotten married and moved away, so they didn't see him often.

Fortunately, Jeremy spotted her, so he waited until she could reach them. Jacob leaned over to hug her. "I heard you were doing great," he said. Then he whispered, "You've got my baby brother doing all kinds of things I never thought he'd do."

Cindi thought that was a curious comment. "Like what?"

"Like considering getting into the wedding business."

"Oh." He obviously hadn't told anyone his change of plans. And she hadn't yet gotten around to telling Fran she wanted to withdraw her listing. "I'm not so sure that's what he really wants."

Jacob offered a conspiratorial grin. "I'm positive that's not what he really wants."

Cindi quickly grew very uncomfortable, and she wanted to change the direction of the conversation. "So how are things with you and your wife?"

He cleared his throat and shook his head. "I'm divorced. I've moved back home until I figure out what to do next."

She felt awful. "I'm so sorry—I had no idea."

"I know. Don't worry about it. Just don't make a stupid mistake like I did and think love conquers all."

Jeremy slipped between them and took over the conversation. "We're going to lunch. Want to join us?"

"No, that's okay," she said. "I have other plans. Let's talk later."

The rest of the afternoon, Cindi did a few things she didn't have time to do during the week. Once everything was finished, she went to visit her mother. Her father had just left.

"I was hoping to catch the two of you together," Cindi said. "Why isn't he staying here?"

"We're taking it very slowly," her mother replied. "I think he'll be moving back by the end of the month, though. The counselor has really helped. If you ever decide to get married, I'd highly suggest getting Christian counseling beforehand. That way you can nip problems in the bud before they start."

"Good thinking," Cindi agreed. "From what I've heard, most pastors do premarital counseling these days before they'll perform the ceremony."

"I wish they'd done that back when your father and I got married. We had so many unrealistic expectations that caused problems later on, it's a wonder we stuck it out as long as we did. We still have a couple more counseling sessions, because there are still some issues we haven't resolved."

Cindi heard that, but she chose to assume everything would be just fine. Both of her parents had taken the steps they needed to keep their marriage together, so what could go wrong?

The following week Cindi was faced with all sorts of problems, starting Monday. One of the weddings she'd put quite a bit of time into had been canceled. The groom got cold feet and said he changed his mind, so the bride and her entire wedding party wanted to cancel their orders.

Then the next day one of the brides she'd worked with a couple of years earlier walked in wanting another wedding gown—only this time she wanted tea length because she didn't think it was appropriate to wear a long white gown for a second wedding. Cindi and Elizabeth listened to her go on and on about how different this marriage would be because they were signing prenuptial agreements and they were each keeping their own residence in case things didn't work out.

After she left, Elizabeth shook her head. "How sad for her. She still doesn't know what marriage is all about."

It seemed as though each day brought even more bad news. Within two weeks, Cindi was once again doubting the business she'd once loved. Her emotions were still on edge and very tender.

"Don't let it get you down," Elizabeth said. "Look at your parents. They're working things out."

"Maybe so, but they're still not living together. Apparently my dad isn't sure reconciling is in their best interest. I think he likes seeing my mom but remaining on his own."

"That's silly," Elizabeth said. "What does their counselor say?"

"I wish I knew. Mom's starting to get depressed about it. I think she's even worse off now than she was before they started trying to get back together."

That night her mother called crying. "This is so hard, Cindi. I can't go on like this. I hate living in a state of limbo, not knowing if we'll ever figure out where we went wrong."

Nothing Cindi said could pull her mother out of her depression. The hope she'd had just a few weeks ago went up in a puff of smoke.

The next morning, Cindi stormed into the shop, dropped her purse into the file cabinet, and slammed it shut. "That's it. I'm selling this place. I was right before. A good marriage is just an image."

"Come on, Cindi," Elizabeth begged. "You can't really mean it. At least give it another year or two."

"Nope. I'm getting out while I'm still young enough to find something else, and I don't want to waste another day." She paused to take a breath before adding, "I'm calling Fran to let her know Jeremy can have it—that is, if he's still interested. I might have blown my only chance to get out. At least now I'm convinced Jeremy is on the up-and-up. If he says he'll personally run the shop, then that's what I believe he'll do."

eleven

Jeremy pulled the cell phone out of his pocket, saw it was Fran, and answered it. Fran didn't even bother identifying herself. Instead, she blurted, "Cindi's changed her mind, and she wants to sell you her shop."

"She what?"

"I think you heard right. She said she'll sell the shop to you, and the sooner the better."

"Wait a minute—let me get this straight. Just a couple of weeks ago, she wanted to keep it."

"Yes," Fran said, "I know. So if you still want the shop, you need to act quickly before she changes her mind again."

Cindi was an intelligent woman, so something had obviously happened. He told Fran he'd get back to her by the end of the day after he had some time to think about it.

Immediately after he flipped the phone shut, he started to call Cindi. But before he pushed the SEND button, he changed his mind. He needed to think before reacting. This situation called for something he could count on. He lowered his head and closed his eyes in prayer.

Lord, give me guidance in what to do about this Cindi thing. Granted, her shop is exactly the type of business I'm looking for, but You know I don't want to take advantage of a weak time in her life. If she's meant to keep the place, show her. Make it clear to her. If You want me to have it, then make that clear, as well.

When he opened his eyes, he knew he needed to be patient and pay attention to the answer. The times he'd gone about his business without regard to what he knew the Lord wanted him to do, things had gone awry.

He had business to tie up in Macon, and he wouldn't be back in Atlanta until late in the evening. The manager of his tire store had turned in his resignation the day before, so he was interviewing new candidates. Fortunately, the two very capable assistant managers could run the place without him, and only one of them wanted the lead position. Jeremy planned to promote him and give the other one a raise for doing such a good job of supporting the business. However, he still had a position to fill, and the candidate pool wasn't as deep as it had been the last time he'd needed someone.

At the end of the day, he hadn't found anyone who seemed capable of filling the very big shoes of the assistant manager he was promoting, but he needed to get back to Atlanta. His employees assured him they'd be fine without him, and he had confidence in them.

He left the tire store in Macon at four thirty hoping to get to his parents' place by dinnertime. Normally the drive back to Atlanta took less than two hours, but traffic was slow. He pulled into the driveway after dark and knew his parents would have finished eating by now. Knowing his mother, though, she'd have a plate filled with leftovers ready for him to microwave.

He was right. The instant he walked into the condo, his mother let him know she was worried. "You should have called," she said.

Back when he was a younger man, her fussing annoyed him. Now, however, her concern touched him deeply. "Yes, I know, and I should have. Sorry. I'll do better next time."

She smiled at him. "You're a good boy, Jeremy. I'm proud of who you've become."

After dinner he went up to his room and placed a call to Cindi's house phone. When she didn't answer, he tried her cell phone. Still no answer.

When Cindi heard the house phone ring, she sank lower into the tub of bubbles. Whoever it was could leave a message, and she'd get back to them when she was finished with her much-needed, relaxing bubble bath. Then her cell phone rang immediately afterward. Maybe it was an emergency.

Knowing she couldn't get to it in time, she slowly rose from the tub, dried off, and wrapped her robe around her. She picked up her cell phone and checked the caller ID. It was Jeremy. She punched in the voice mail number and listened. He said she needed to call him back as soon as she got the message. What could he possibly want that was important enough to call her now?

She toyed with the thought of waiting until the next day to return his call. But what if it really was important?

She got into her pajamas then called his number. He picked up before the end of the first ring.

"Why are you selling the shop?" he asked. "I thought you decided to keep it."

"Is that why you called, Jeremy?"

"Yes. I'm worried about you."

"Do you want it or not?" she asked, trying to ignore how his voice made her feel inside.

"Before I answer that, we need to talk. I'm not about to take something away from you that you need to keep."

Cindi sighed. "Look, Jeremy, it's not up to you to decide what I need to keep. I just had a change of heart, and I've decided my first instinct to sell was what I should have stuck with."

"What happened?"

She didn't want to tell him the details. "I prayed for guidance, and let's just say I got it."

"So you had a setback, huh?"

"More than a setback." Cindi felt herself growing impatient. "Look, Jeremy, I don't want to have to explain every single decision I make. Do you want the shop or not?"

He paused long enough to rattle her. "I'm not sure now. I've been praying, too, and it's not clear to me yet."

Cindi couldn't respond to that immediately. If they were both praying for guidance and they were getting different answers, what did that mean?

Finally, she knew she had to say something. "Then I'll just put it back on the market and let things fall into place."

"With prayer."

"That goes without saying."

She heard him sigh. "If you truly want to sell, I'd like to take you up on your offer and buy it. I'll get with Fran and resubmit my offer."

Cindi felt sick to her stomach. She mumbled a few words then told him she needed to go.

After she got off the phone, Cindi's emotions swirled. She went from being confused to angry to remorseful. Although she was now fairly certain she wanted to sell, doubts still tugged at the back of her mind and heart.

❧

Even though Jeremy doubted Cindi really wanted to sell, all he could think about now was Cindi selling her shop to the wrong person. She'd been worried about him coming in and working the bottom line at the expense of her precious store's integrity. What he did was nothing compared to what he'd seen out there in the business world.

He'd watched successful businesses get milked and then squeezed for the last dime of profit before the profiteer boarded the doors and sent employees scurrying to the unemployment line. Jeremy had never done that—not even once. In fact, in some cases he'd built businesses then sold them to the employees with a generous payback plan. It sickened him to watch others get taken advantage of.

He needed to figure out what had happened to change Cindi's mind and send her back to the Realtor. Her passion for life—the same passion that had attracted him to her in the first place—was the exact same thing that put the spark in what she did with her clients.

Cindi had always been a Christian. Now her love for the Lord gave her a quiet confidence that came through in everything she did—except in one area: her confusion about what to do with her boutique. He had to find out what was going on to make her change her mind so quickly.

In the meantime he called Fran, who advised him not to submit an offer he didn't want to go through with. "She's a very motivated seller now," Fran said. "I have to admit, I'll be glad when she makes up her mind. The other folks in my office are advising me to pull out of the listing, but I'm afraid she'd be taken advantage of by someone else if I did that."

As difficult as it was, Jeremy knew he couldn't pursue this until he got to the heart of the matter. "Let's just hold off for a few days. Hopefully she won't get any more offers until she has time to decide what she really wants to do."

Fran paused then said, "You're quite a man, Jeremy. The Lord has blessed you, and you've honored your faith."

❧

When Fran called Cindi and told her Jeremy was holding back his offer, she wasn't surprised, but she was very annoyed. As soon as she got off the phone, she told Elizabeth what had happened.

Elizabeth shook her head. "I wonder what Jeremy's game is. If he really wanted this place, you practically just handed it to him."

"I don't know. He seems to think I'm supposed to keep this place."

"That's one area where I agree with him," Elizabeth said. "But I'm not so sure we have the same motives."

"Does that really matter?"

"Yes, it absolutely does," Elizabeth stated firmly. "And you know it, too. If he's backing out because he truly feels you're supposed to keep this shop, that's one thing. However, if he's trying to pull away from the sale to get you to lower your price, then he's nothing but a. . .a. . ." She cleared her throat.

"Don't say it," Cindi said. "I know what you're thinking."

"Well, I suspect his motives aren't as pure and holy as he'd like you to believe. Going to church doesn't make him a good guy."

"True, but after he explained things, I don't think he was ever a bad guy."

Elizabeth lifted her hands in a gesture of exasperation. "How can you be so nice after what he did to you? I remember you cried for days."

Cindi nodded. "Yeah, the breakup hurt me pretty badly."

"And if I remember correctly, he didn't exactly let you down easy. What he said was harsh." Elizabeth tilted her head forward and looked at Cindi from beneath hooded eyes. "What he did then is similar to now, only then it was his love he pulled back. Now it's the offer to buy this place."

Looking down at the floor, Cindi mentally rehashed the scene that had played over and over in her mind for months. Back in high school, Jeremy had told her he loved her every time they were together, and then one day, out of the blue, he said he didn't love her anymore and he wanted his ring back. She begged him to tell her what she'd done, but he never came out and gave her any specifics. He just said they weren't meant to be together. She asked if he'd found another girl, and he shrugged, saying there were lots of other girls. His comment made her sick to her stomach, so she'd run away. Even his explanation about giving her up so she could have the freedom to pursue her dream and go to college seemed lame now.

With a deep sigh, Cindi nodded. "You're right, it was harsh. But we were kids then."

"You know that old saying about a leopard's spots."

Cindi nodded. "There's some merit to that, unless a person has truly accepted Christ. In that case, the saying doesn't count."

"But why take chances with something as important to you as this shop? Maybe Jeremy has changed, and he's a wonderful Christian guy with the best of intentions. But then again, maybe he's the same old person who takes advantage of other people. An opportunist." She paused before adding, "How would you feel if you sold it to him and then a year later he closed the doors after draining all the profit?"

She'd feel as though someone had twisted a knife inside her. "You've thought about this a lot, haven't you?"

Elizabeth nodded. "Yes, I'm afraid so. It not only affects you; it matters to me."

"I'm sure you can find another job."

"Of course I can, but it won't be the same. However, it's not the job I'm talking about. It's more that I'll have to watch you suffer."

The more Cindi listened to Elizabeth, the more convicted she was to wait just a little while—at least until she had a clearer idea of what she needed to do, or Jeremy decided to move on to something else.

"It does seem a little strange that he spent so much time trying to woo me. I assumed he was still interested in the business—especially after what you heard in Fran's office. But immediately after I offer to let him buy it, he reminds me that he's changed his mind," Cindi admitted.

"Yeah, it doesn't sound right to me."

"I don't understand what he'll gain from this, and I don't want to think he's playing games, but still. . ." She lifted one shoulder then let it drop. "I have to admit, I'm a little confused. He just needs to be straight up about what he wants."

"That's right. You have too much self-respect for that, and you're too smart to let him keep pulling stunts to get what he wants."

A bride and her mother came in, so they turned all their attention to their customers. They were almost finished when the phone rang. Elizabeth answered it, so Cindi scheduled the next appointment for the bridesmaids to come in for their fittings. Elizabeth didn't rejoin them, which aroused Cindi's curiosity.

After the customers left, Cindi went directly to where Elizabeth stood. "Who called?"

Elizabeth looked at her and shook her head. "Jeremy. He said he needed to talk to you, and I told him to quit bothering you. This is taking up way too much of your time and energy."

"Yeah, but—"

"Don't go soft on him," Elizabeth warned. "He knows how to get what he wants, and if he's playing the game we think he's playing, we need to let him know we're not falling into it."

"Exactly what did he say?" Cindi asked.

"He asked if you were in. That's when I told him to back off."

"That's all he said?"

"Yup. I wasn't about to give him a chance—"

Elizabeth was interrupted by the door opening, and they both looked up.

"Jeremy," Cindi said softly.

He wasn't looking at her. Instead, his gaze fixed on Elizabeth. "Why did you hang up on me?" he asked.

Cindi snapped around to see Elizabeth's reaction. Elizabeth

shrugged as she played with the rubber band in her hands. "We don't have time for games," she mumbled.

Jeremy turned to Cindi. "Do you think I'm playing games?"

His direct question caught Cindi off guard. In fact, this whole situation made her want to run and hide. But she had to face him and admit her thoughts, or this kind of encounter would never end.

"I don't know what to think," Cindi replied. She could see Elizabeth glaring at her from the corner of her eye, but she ignored it. "I thought you'd want to buy the place if I agreed to it. It doesn't seem right."

Jeremy rested an elbow on the counter and turned to Elizabeth, who'd remained in the same position, scowling, since he arrived. "So tell me what you think I'm up to."

Elizabeth took a step toward them. "In sales it's called the takeaway close. People want what they can't have."

Cindi turned to Jeremy, who looked perplexed. "Have you ever heard of that?"

He nodded. "I'm familiar with the takeaway close, but I can assure you that's not what I was doing."

"Then what were you doing?" Elizabeth asked, fist planted firmly on her hip.

Cindi turned to her. "Thanks, Elizabeth, but I can handle this."

Elizabeth backed away and held up her hands in surrender. "Okay, okay, I'll be in the sewing room if you need me."

After she left, Jeremy turned back to Cindi. "She really cares about you. It's nice to have a friend who's willing to stick up for you like that."

"Yes, I know."

"But I'm afraid she has it all wrong. Cindi, I know I've been a jerk in the past, but I've completely changed. I'd never want to hurt you in any way, which is why I'm backing off." When he paused, Cindi thought he looked like a tortured man. "I've prayed about the right thing to do, and I think it's obvious you're exactly where you should be with this shop. I need to go find something else to buy."

"Go buy whatever you want," Cindi said. "Just don't try to tell me what I should or shouldn't do."

Jeremy closed his eyes for a few seconds. Cindi wondered if he was praying; he certainly looked as though he was.

When he opened his eyes, they focused directly on her. "I would never tell you what you should do. What I'm saying is I don't want to get involved in something that would ever hurt you or upset you in any way. . .again. I thought you understood that."

Cindi's mouth went dry. She felt that old aching sensation in her chest—the one that had faded since he'd broken her heart.

"Ever since I put my faith in the Lord, my business practices have changed." He paused and cleared his throat. "Everything about me has changed. I pray for guidance when I first wake up. I end my days in prayer, and I fill in every moment possible with prayer. The Lord has been good to me, even when I was hardheaded."

There was no mistaking the conviction in Jeremy's voice as he spoke of his faith. She'd been wrong to jump to conclusions. Her pain shifted to an emotion she'd never felt before. It was a connection to the man standing before her, but it was much deeper than the attraction that was there years ago.

"I've grown in many ways because of my faith," he continued. "Emotionally, mentally, and even physically. I never want to forget my blessings, and I honor all He's given me." As he took a step closer, Cindi's heart hammered in her chest. "And I want with all my heart for you to believe me. I care about you more than I ever did."

twelve

After Jeremy left, Elizabeth appeared in the showroom. "So what all did he say to get you to sell him your shop?"

Cindi moved toward the door and looked out to avoid squaring off with Elizabeth. "He didn't even try."

"Ooh, he's smooth."

"He really doesn't want to buy it now," Cindi said as she turned around and faced Elizabeth.

"And you believe him?"

Cindi nodded. "Yes, I do."

Elizabeth looked frustrated, but she quickly recovered. "Then why don't you tell me what happened, and we can try to figure it out."

"No, I really don't want to try to figure anything out—at least not what concerns Jeremy. I just want to know what I should do about this place."

"You know how I feel," Elizabeth said. "This bridal shop is the perfect fit for you."

"It goes much deeper than that," Cindi said. "But I don't want to discuss it anymore. Let's get back to work."

As the day wore on, Cindi's mind kept drifting back to her conversation with Jeremy. His last sentence kept playing through her mind until she knew she had to find out exactly what he meant by that. She'd never completely gotten over the breakup, but until now she'd figured she'd just have to live with him in her past. But he said he cared about her more than ever.

About an hour before closing time, Elizabeth approached her at the desk. "You've been distracted all day, and after your conversation with Jeremy, I can understand. Why don't you go on home? I can close up."

Cindi nodded. "I think I will. Thanks." She gathered her belongings and headed home.

Being alone only escalated her thoughts, so finally she decided she needed to call and ask Jeremy exactly what he meant. If he was sincere about his faith, he wouldn't mind. And if he wasn't sincere, what did she care about what he thought?

She called his cell phone, but he didn't answer. Maybe he was at his parents' house. After a brief hesitation, she looked up their number and called.

"He's in Savannah." It wasn't Jeremy or his dad. "Who's this?"

"Cindi Clark," she replied. "Is this Jacob?"

His voice instantly softened. "Hey, Cindi. Yeah, this is Jacob."

"Um. . .do you know when Jeremy will be back?"

"He had some business to take care of in Savannah, and it might take awhile. Is this an emergency?"

"No, it's not an emergency, but would you mind letting him know I called?"

"I'll be glad to," Jacob said. "Jeremy hasn't stopped talking about you since I've been here."

"Um. . ." She had no idea how to respond.

"I'll have Jeremy call you when I hear from him."

"Thanks."

"It was nice talking to you, Cindi."

After she hung up, Cindi found herself reading between the lines and wondering what all had been said about her.

❧

The cell phone went off in Jeremy's pocket, so he pulled it out to see who it was. The call was from his parents' house, so he excused himself and answered it.

"Hey, bro. You might want to wrap things up quickly and head on back."

Jeremy took another step back from the counter of the men's clothing store where he'd been talking to Brad, the manager, about buying the place. "Why? What happened? Are Mom and Dad okay?"

"They're fine. I just heard from your woman."

"My woman? Which one?" Jeremy was used to his brother, so he played along.

"Seriously, dude, I'm talking about Cindi. She just called here."

"What did she say?"

"She wanted to know when you'd be back. I asked her if it was an emergency, and she said it wasn't, so don't worry. I just think you need to know she wants to talk to you."

"Okay, I'll call her. Thanks for letting me know."

"One more thing. . ."

"What's that?"

"Don't let her get away again. And you know what I'm talkin' about."

Jeremy didn't even try to pretend. "Yes, I do know. Thanks."

He told the manager of the store he'd be back soon before stepping outside. Tourists passed him as they headed toward the shopping district on River Street a block away. He'd seen the unrealized potential of this menswear store a couple of years earlier, so he'd walked in, made an offer, and owned the business a month later. With a strong Web presence and referrals from the Chamber of Commerce and River Street Association, he'd tripled the profits. And now it was time to sell so he could focus on his move back to Atlanta.

He opened his flip phone, found Cindi's number, and pressed SEND. She answered immediately.

"You didn't have to call me right back," she said. "I told

Jacob it wasn't an emergency."

"Did you need something?"

There was a long pause before she finally said, "Yeah, I wanted to know what was going on with you. Even after you said you didn't want to buy my place, I thought you were just changing your game." She cleared her throat before adding, "And that part about caring for me more now than before. . . well, never mind."

He was a little surprised she came right out and said that. "I meant it."

"It doesn't matter. What we had as kids was just a high school crush anyway."

"Not for me," he said quickly. Should he have admitted that? Maybe not, but it was done now, and he didn't regret it. "I was hoping you'd feel. . .well, you know."

"I'm not sure of anything anymore."

"I. . ." What was the right thing to say now? He glanced around at the people strolling past him and decided it would be best to take up this conversation again in person. "Tell you what, Cindi. I'd like to talk some more so we can get this thing resolved. Why don't we get together when I get back and lay everything on the table?"

"Okay, that's fine with me."

After they hung up, Jeremy sucked in a deep breath and slowly let it out before going back inside to finish his discussion with the manager. He loved Savannah, but he loved being home in the Atlanta area even more. However, now that he was here, he planned to enjoy a few of his favorite things.

Jeremy was hungry as usual, so he decided to stop off at one of his favorite eating places—a well-known former boarding-house that had turned into a country-style restaurant—where he could get his fill of some of the finest Southern cook-ing he'd ever tasted. One of the servers,

Bonnie, told him he looked anxious.

"I'm not anxious. Just eager to get home."

She offered a wide grin. "Must be a pretty girl."

No point in arguing. "Absolutely. What else could it be?"

"You'd better let her know how you feel, 'cause from what I've seen, if a girl can make you want to run back to see her, there's other fellas wantin' to do the same thing."

"Thanks, Bonnie. I'll try to remember that."

"After she says yes, bring her back here so I can see what got my favorite customer so in a flutter."

"Says yes?"

She planted her fist on her hip and shook her head. "Some men can be so dense. Don't let her get away. Get to know her real good, find out what's in her heart. See if she loves Jesus, and if you still feel this way, you'd better walk that girl down the aisle."

He nearly choked on his corn bread. "Got any more sweet tea?"

"Sure thing." Bonnie walked away from the table laughing.

He paid his tab and left, feeling a mixture of confusion and anticipation. His conversation with Bonnie had made him think.

As he drove past rows of Victorian houses and antique stores, Jeremy thought about what a fabulous honeymoon destination Savannah would be. He passed one of the historic squares where a couple sat on a bench laughing and snuggling. A warm feeling traveled from his head to his toes, and he knew he wanted more out of life than what he currently had.

Lord, if it's Your will, give me the strength to share my feelings with Cindi. And give me even more strength to deal with her response.

The drive home seemed to take forever, but he finally arrived in his parents' driveway at dinnertime. When he walked inside, his mother said dinner was being served in a few minutes.

"Thanks, Mom, but I'm going to see if Cindi wants to go out."

She grinned. "I would tell you to invite her over, but I think the two of you need to be alone."

Am I that obvious? He guessed so.

Cindi was still at the shop when he called, and she said she still had quite a bit to do. "Elizabeth just had pizza delivered so we can finish up here. Why don't we talk later? Can you come to my place around eight?"

At least she wasn't pushing him away. "I'll be there at eight on the dot."

He told his mother, so she handed him a plate. "Set yourself a place, and we'll eat together as a family—just like old times."

When they sat down, Jeremy was happy his father bowed his head, then looked up and told everyone else to do the same. His brother winked and bowed his head. Their father finished the very short blessing, thanking the Lord for the meal. This gave Jeremy hope for even more great things to come.

At exactly seven forty-five, he left for Cindi's place. She opened the door before he had a chance to knock.

"So what did you want to talk about?" she asked.

No point in beating around the bush. "Us."

She blinked, and her face turned red. "Okay, come on in and have a seat."

He followed her into the living room that had been tastefully decorated with what he remembered were her favorite colors: peach and green. She had a couple of live plants flanking a small entertainment center across from a tan sectional sofa with peach and green pillows in various patterns and prints. "Your place looks really nice, Cindi."

"Thanks." She sat down and looked around the room. He could tell she was nervous.

"I don't want to play games anymore, Cindi," he began, "so I might as well get straight to the point. I fell in love with you back in high school, and the feeling never went away. I couldn't hold you back in good conscience. There were so many things you wanted that I couldn't give you at the time."

"But I didn't want anything," she said softly, "except you."

"We've been down that road before. You know I was a confused, broken kid with no idea what was in my future."

"I never cared about money," she said. "I thought you knew that about me."

He could hear the pain in her voice. "I didn't want to hurt you, Cindi, but it was the only way I knew to make going away to college easy for you."

She didn't say a word. Instead, she looked away, shaking her head.

"But things have changed now, and I have quite a bit more to offer—namely, my faith. I just hope it isn't too late."

She slowly turned to face him. "I'm not sure, Jeremy. I was hurt very badly, and it'll take a long time for me to learn to completely trust you again." She fidgeted with the edge of the cushion. "I have to admit, I still have feelings, and I believe you when you say you have faith in God. It's just that, well, I don't want to put myself in a vulnerable position."

"I understand that. All I ask is that you give me time. I'll do whatever it takes. I've even sold all my out-of-town businesses so I can focus all my energy on establishing myself here in Atlanta."

"Let me think about this, okay?" she said.

He stood and walked toward the door. "Thanks, Cindi." She walked toward him, so he instinctively reached for her hand.

She paused then took his hand in hers. He squeezed, and she offered a small grin, which gave him a flicker of hope.

All the way to his parents' house, he thought about ways to win her over. He knew she wouldn't be impressed by fancy restaurants, but he wanted to take her to the finest places. She'd come out and said she wasn't motivated by money, but he wanted to buy her the world. The guys at the tire store had pooled their resources and offered to buy him out. He was glad to help them get started. And now he was in the final stages of selling the men's clothing store. All he had to do was go back for the closing, and then he could turn all his attention toward what was really important.

As difficult as it was, he decided to stay away from her shop for a few days and give her time to think. On Thursday night he got a call from Brad in Savannah. "I finished all the paperwork, and I've been approved. The bank said we can sign off on the paperwork tomorrow morning. We can handle it by mail and I'll be the owner by the end of next week, or if you can be here tomorrow, we can be done with it."

"I'll be there first thing in the morning," Jeremy said. There was no reason to put it off.

❧

Friday morning after she got to the shop, Cindi decided to call Jeremy and see if he could come over that night. She'd thought about what she wanted, and it was clear after not seeing him since their heart-to-heart talk that she wanted the same thing he said he wanted. She tried his cell phone first, but he didn't answer, so she called his parents' house.

Again, Jacob answered the phone. "Seems like every time you call, my brother's in Savannah at his store."

His store? Had he lied when he told her he'd sold all his businesses?

"Want me to give him a message?" Jacob asked.

"N–no, that's okay."

After she hung up, she saw Elizabeth watching her from

across the room. She tried to busy herself with some papers, but she knew she couldn't fool her best friend.

"Okay, what gives?" Elizabeth asked. "What did Jeremy do this time?"

Cindi fought the tears as she shrugged. "He's back in Savannah at *his shop*."

Elizabeth lifted one eyebrow. "His shop, huh? Well, that pretty much lets you know how much you can trust him, doesn't it?"

The tears suddenly took control and streamed down Cindi's cheeks. She couldn't stop them. Elizabeth wasted no time in coming over to her and pulling her into an embrace.

"How could I have been so wrong to trust him?" Cindi asked. "Why did he tell me he'd sold everything when he still had a place in Savannah?"

"Who knows why Jeremy Hayden does anything?" Elizabeth said.

"He said he wanted to settle down in Atlanta, and that was just a few days ago."

"Something still doesn't seem right."

The phone rang. When Elizabeth hesitated, Cindi nodded for her to answer it.

Based on Elizabeth's side of the conversation, she gathered there had been a mix-up of some dress measurements, which would require some last-minute scrambling on their part. After Elizabeth got off the phone, both of them sprang into action.

Her tears dried as she managed to deal with the distraction. As much of a hassle as it was, she was glad it happened. This disaster turned out to be a blessing to keep her busy.

However, the rest of the day only grew worse. Another of her former customers stopped by to say hi and to let her know the marriage didn't even last a year. Her mother later called and said her father was so wrapped up in his job that he'd missed a counseling session. By closing time, Cindi wanted to crawl into a hole and never come out.

"Wanna go see a movie?" Elizabeth asked. "There's a new action flick playing, and I figure it'll get your mind off everything else."

"No, that's okay."

"I don't want you to be alone when you're this upset. Want me to come over to your place for a little while?"

"I appreciate your concern, but this is one time I probably need to be alone. I have to sort out some of my thoughts."

"Are you sure?"

Cindi nodded. "Positive. I'll be fine."

She headed home and dropped her purse in the kitchen. Then she grabbed her Bible and sat on the couch in the living room, where she flipped to some places she'd marked over the past several weeks during church. A quiet peace came over her as she realized she'd been neglecting this very important part of her life and trying to make things go the way she thought they should.

When her phone rang, she got up to answer it. When she saw it was Jeremy, she backed away. Now wasn't a good time to talk to him—not when she was still reeling over his lies.

After more than an hour of reading her Bible, she bowed her head in prayer. She asked for guidance in her decision about not only Jeremy but also her shop. It was time to stop worrying about selling the business and focus more on her walk with the Lord.

thirteen

"You totally won't believe this," Elizabeth said as she stormed out of the fitting room where a bride was being fitted. "They sent the wrong size."

Cindi tilted her head to one side. "Can't you fix it?"

Elizabeth's eyes widened, and she held out her hands, palms up. "Not this time. The dress is, like, two sizes too small."

Cindi groaned. "This is the same vendor we've been having all the problems with. Well, I guess this will be the last time we use them."

"In the meantime, we have to get this girl a dress."

"Okay, tell her I'll be right there. Let me make a quick phone call."

As soon as Elizabeth went back into the fitting room, Cindi called all the vendors she knew would work with her. Armed with half a dozen brochures and a few more samples, she knocked on the fitting room door. The bride, Marisa, was sitting hunched over on a chair, a blanket wrapped around her, looking stunned and on the verge of tears.

It was time to pull out all the stops. "I have some dresses you'll like even more," Cindi said. "This one retails for about 20 percent more than the other one sells for, and I'll let you have it for the same price."

Marisa looked at the dress. "Will you be able to get it for me in time for the wedding?"

"Absolutely," Cindi said. "In case you don't like that one, I have others. I'll see to it that you have the wedding dress of your dreams."

She tried on all the dresses Cindi brought into the room, and she chose one that she liked even more than her original one. It was quite a bit more expensive, but Cindi wasn't about to let that be a deal breaker. "Like I told you, I'm not charging a dime more. They can overnight it, and you can be fitted tomorrow." Cindi saw the look of panic in her eyes. "Or if you don't mind taking a sample, I'll let you have this dress with an extra 10 percent discount."

"You'll do that?" Marisa said with a smile.

Cindi and Elizabeth exchanged a glance and nodded. "It's my job to help make your wedding day be one of the best days of your life."

As soon as Marisa left, Cindi called the vendor, thanked the woman for her willingness to work with them, then told her she'd sold the sample to the bride. Afterward she flopped onto the love seat by the front desk. "That was a nightmare."

Elizabeth sat down across from her. "Ya know, I sort of enjoyed being part of fixing the problem. Not everyone in our position would have helped her like we did."

Cindi thought about it, nodded, and smiled. "Yeah, you're right. It feels really good to be a problem solver in the eleventh hour."

Elizabeth held up one hand. "High five?"

Cindi slapped her friend's hand. "Okay, now it's time to get back to work. We have another appointment in an hour, and you need to start the alterations on that dress. I'll straighten up the fitting room."

"What do you plan to do with the dress she ordered?" Elizabeth asked as they stood up. "The one that didn't fit."

Cindi shrugged. "I guess I'll send it back."

"It's a gorgeous dress."

"I agree. Too bad it was the wrong size."

Elizabeth stood there as though she wanted to say something, but she didn't say a word. Cindi wasn't sure what her friend was thinking, so she decided to break the silence.

"Why don't you try it on?"

Elizabeth's eyes lit up. "Great idea!" She glanced up at the clock. "We still have awhile before our next appointment. Mind if I do it now?"

Cindi gestured toward the fitting room. "Be my guest."

"I'll need you to zip it for me."

"Just holler when you're ready."

A few minutes later when Cindi didn't hear a peep out of the fitting room, she edged a little closer. She heard the swishing sound of a dress.

"Is it on yet?"

"It doesn't fit," Elizabeth called back. "I'm too bony for a dress like this."

"Bummer. I was looking forward to seeing it on you. It's one of the prettiest dresses I've ever seen."

"Then why don't you try it on?" Elizabeth said.

"No way."

"And why not?" Elizabeth said. "Afraid?"

"No, I'm not afraid," Cindi said as she tried to laugh it off. "I just don't see any point in trying on a dress I'll never wear."

"So what? It's pretty. What's the harm in trying it on?"

Elizabeth stood at the door of the fitting room straightening her top. She pointed to the dress she'd hung on the rack behind her.

"I think it'll look great on you. The bodice is fitted, but the skirt has a graceful flare, just like what you always said you liked."

Cindi looked at the dress on the hanger. It was truly one of the prettiest dresses she'd ever seen, with simple but elegant lines, the high scoop neck just low enough to wear a necklace without being self-conscious, a cascade of pearl beading down the front, and off-shoulder sleeves.

With a shrug, Cindi turned away. "I just don't think I need to get in the habit of trying on the merchandise."

"We used to do it all the time," Elizabeth reminded her.

"That was a long time ago. I don't want to do that anymore."

"Chicken." Elizabeth added a few clucking sounds for effect.

Cindi clicked her tongue and edged past Elizabeth. "Oh, all right, I'll try it on. I'll call you when it's time to zip me up."

After Elizabeth left the fitting room and closed the door, Cindi stood and stared at the dress. It really was a gorgeous gown. Finally, she inhaled deeply, blew out her breath, and undressed. As she stepped into the wedding gown, an odd sensation washed over her. It was a combination of anticipation and dread, because at the rate things were going, this would be the only way she'd try on a dress.

She stood in front of the mirror and stared at the dress for a couple of minutes before she heard Elizabeth outside the door. "Are you ready?"

"Almost."

"What's taking you so long?"

"Okay, you can come in now," Cindi finally said.

Elizabeth's eyes widened as she stepped inside the room. "You look absolutely stunning. This dress was made for you."

Cindi couldn't say anything for several seconds. Rarely did a dress fit perfectly. Sometimes all a bride needed was a simple tuck or a hem, but a fit like this had only happened a couple of times in all the years she'd owned this place.

If she ever got married, this was the dress she'd have to have. There wasn't even a close second.

As Cindi looked away from the mirror and toward her friend, she knew what Elizabeth was thinking. "Unzip me."

Elizabeth did as she was told. Neither of them said a word until the dress was hung back up and they were out on the sales floor.

"Are you okay?" Elizabeth asked softly.

Cindi nodded as a lump formed in her throat. She coughed then turned the page of the appointment book and pointed to the next entry. "I have a feeling this one will be difficult. The bride's bringing her mother and the groom's mother."

Elizabeth groaned. "I'm not in the mood for a bridal meltdown."

With a chuckle, Cindi nodded. "I know what you mean, but tending to bridal meltdowns is one of the things we do best."

The threesome was difficult and required all their tact and energy, but between the two of them, they managed without breaking stride. The bride, Ginger, let them know what she wanted from the beginning, so they slanted their presentation in her direction.

When it appeared the mother-of-the-bride and mother-of-the-groom were growing restless, Elizabeth looked at Cindi, who nodded. It was time for them to spring into action.

"Hey, moms," Elizabeth said in her most enthusiastic voice. "I think we have some great gowns that'll look fabulous on both of you." She pulled one off the rack and held it up. "This comes in almost all the color selections, and it's flattering on most women."

The mothers turned all their attention to Elizabeth while Cindi got information from the bride on what she was looking for in a dress. While Elizabeth helped the mothers, she found Ginger a strapless gown with a sleek A-line and very little embellishment—just like she'd wanted.

"I have a necklace and earrings from my grandmother, so this will be perfect."

"Oh, I agree," Cindi said. "Let's get you set up in fitting room one. I can find a couple more, just in case you don't like the way this one fits. Just don't think you have to make your final decision today."

"I don't want to waste your time," Ginger said.

"You won't be wasting my time. I'd much rather have you come back in a more relaxed mood and get a dress that'll make you happy." Cindi smiled at her. "And perhaps you'll only want to bring your mom next time."

Ginger giggled. "Sounds good to me."

After the mothers settled on their gowns, Ginger was ready for them to see her. Even the groom's mother agreed the dress she chose was stunning.

"My son will be so happy when he sees you walking down the aisle." The woman's eyes glistened with tears, and Ginger's mother reached out and rubbed her back.

The scene was so touching that Cindi had to look away. She saw Elizabeth starting to tear up.

Cindi nodded. "When you put on that dress, it was obvious that was the one." She'd seen brides' eyes light up as they stepped into the dress they loved more than all the rest. "It didn't take long at all to find it, either."

They scheduled future appointments for the bride and her mother to come back for her first fitting, and then for the groom's mother to come in with the bride's mother for their gowns. Ginger said she wanted to wait until the moms had their dresses picked out before she brought the bridesmaids.

After they left, Cindi gave Elizabeth a thumbs-up. "Good job."

"As always," Elizabeth agreed.

Cindi looked toward the fitting room where the dress she'd tried on still hung on the hook. Each time she looked at it, she felt an unfamiliar tug at her heart.

"Go try it on again," Elizabeth urged. "You have plenty of time." She smiled at Cindi. "I can tell you really want to."

There was no point in arguing, because Cindi knew she was transparent. "Okay, but just once more."

"But first, let me get a necklace and veil to go with it," Elizabeth said.

Elizabeth helped her into the gown and wouldn't let her turn toward the mirrors until she had the jewelry and veil in place. She held Cindi's hands as she looked her up and down.

"You look even more amazing, girl. No one else can ever wear this dress and do it justice like you do."

"Okay, so I need to turn around and see for myself. That is, if you'll let me have my hands back."

Elizabeth let go of her hands and motioned toward the mirror. "Go ahead."

When Cindi saw her reflection, she let out an involuntary gasp.

fourteen

"Amazing," Elizabeth said. "And stunning."

Cindi was breathless at first, but then reality hit hard. "Stunning for someone who'll never wear the thing." She stepped away from the mirror and backed up to Elizabeth. "Unzip me, please."

After she was out of the gown and back in her work clothes, Cindi shook her head. "Don't let me do that again."

"Do what?" Elizabeth challenged. "See yourself as a blushing bride when you think it's not possible? That's really silly, you know."

"First of all, getting married isn't a guarantee of happiness."

"True." Elizabeth tilted her head and folded her arms without blinking. "So?"

"Secondly, I don't even know a guy I'd want to marry, so it's a moot point."

"Whose fault is that? There are plenty of guys at church who'd love to go out with you."

"Says who?" Cindi said.

"Come on, Cindi. Blake and Andrew have both asked you out."

"Okay, so let's say I'm not interested in them. They're nice and all, but. . ." She shrugged. "As long as I keep this business, I'm not likely to meet many bachelors."

Elizabeth lifted one shoulder and let it drop in a half shrug. "You're selling the place, and you'll eventually have to find a job, so you can look for a place with a nice selection of men."

"Christian men," Cindi reminded her.

"That's fine. Christian men are all over the place. I'm sure you can find someone."

Cindi felt her shoulders sag. "But I can't get past the fact my parents are separated. If they can't make a marriage work, who can?"

"There are plenty of people who make marriage work," Elizabeth said. "Remember a few weeks ago when we celebrated the Siebels' golden anniversary after church? And how about some of the mothers of our brides who have been married a long time?"

"Most of them are divorced and either still single or married to second or third husbands."

"And me," Elizabeth reminded her. "I'm happily married."

Cindi smiled at her. "You're unique."

Elizabeth gently reached out and placed her hand on Cindi's shoulder. "Look, hon, why don't you calm down and not think about this whole divorce thing so much? I know you're heartbroken about your parents' split, but maybe they'll work things out. All you can do is pray for them that they'll find a solution to whatever problem we don't understand."

Cindi finally nodded. "Okay, you're right. I've become such a worrier about my parents, and I know the Lord doesn't want that."

"So go home and get some rest. I'll close up here."

All the way home Cindi thought about Elizabeth's words, and she knew she was right. She really did need to stop worrying about something she couldn't control. As soon as she pulled into her driveway, she bowed her head and asked for peace and the ability to see the blessings rather than the problems.

As she changed into casual clothes, she caught glimpses of herself in the dresser mirror. The memory of how she'd looked in the wedding gown flashed through her mind, and she found herself thinking about how she'd once had hope for finding Mr. Right and floating down the aisle in a gorgeous dress. The only guy she'd ever loved was Jeremy, but he obviously didn't feel the same way. She'd found the dress, but Mr. Right hadn't hung in there for her.

She dumped some salad from a bag into a bowl and topped it with some leftover chicken. This was the extent of her culinary energy at the moment, so she was doing well having a salad.

After she finished most of her salad, she got up and rinsed her bowl. Then the doorbell rang.

She hollered, "Be right there," as she stuck the bowl in the dishwasher and dried her hands on the kitchen towel.

Expecting either Elizabeth or her mother, she was surprised to see Jeremy standing there holding a small bouquet of flowers. "I stopped off at the grocery store on the way here. All the florists were closed."

She shivered with a momentary flash of joy as she stepped aside and let him in. "You didn't have to bring flowers."

"You don't like them?"

"Of course I like them." She took them from him and motioned for him to follow her to the kitchen. She mentally told herself to be aloof and distant or she'd risk showing her feelings. If he'd been honest with her about selling his business in Savannah, she wouldn't have felt this way.

"Have I told you how impressed I am that you've managed to be so successful in business and buy your own place?"

"Thanks." Cindi looked away to keep from letting Jeremy see her cheeks as they heated.

"I'm curious about something. How long have you been in this house?"

"A couple of years. I tried living with my parents after college, but it was hard since I'd been away for four years.

Then I shared an apartment with Elizabeth for three years while I saved for a down payment." *Don't look him in the eye,* she reminded herself.

"You're way ahead of me," he said as he leaned against the counter and watched her arrange the flowers in a small vase. "I have a car and a nice portfolio of businesses I've bought and sold, but that's about it."

"This isn't a competition, Jeremy. Why did you come here?"

"My brother said you called. I tried to call you back, but you never answered."

Cindi shrugged. "I figured there wasn't anything to talk about since you were so busy with *your business* in Savannah." As soon as the words left her mouth, she knew she sounded sarcastic.

He tilted his head and looked at her with a confused expression. "What's wrong, Cindi? What did I do to make you so angry?"

She hadn't wanted to get into a deep discussion with him, but now that he'd come right out and asked, she figured she might as well tell him to clear the air.

"I don't like being lied to."

"Who lied?" he asked. "I don't get it."

"You really don't know, do you?"

"You're right," he replied. "I really don't know."

"I thought you said you'd sold your businesses, but when I called, Jacob said you were at your store in Savannah."

He frowned then pursed his lips. "Okay, so you got me on a technicality. I still officially owned the store until I went to sign the papers turning it over to the manager who bought me out."

"So you don't have any more businesses in Savannah?"

"Nope. I don't own a single business at the moment, and I have to admit it's a little disconcerting. This is the first time since I purchased the candy store that I haven't been a business owner."

Cindi felt a strange sensation in her chest—a combination of relief and embarrassment. "I'm really sorry, Jeremy. I shouldn't have assumed anything."

He reached his hand toward her. "Friends?"

Slowly and as calmly as she could, she accepted his gesture. As their hands touched, she felt the intensity of the moment. She tried to pull away, but he wouldn't let go. So she led him to the living room, where they sat on the sofa but remained silent. Cindi liked being here with him, but she wondered what he was thinking. He stared at her then closed his eyes for a few seconds before looking at her again.

❦

Jeremy couldn't take his eyes off the girl he'd loved for many years. As they sat in silence, he rehashed what he'd learned during the past several hours.

He'd kept the deepest of his feelings to himself, but there wasn't a reason to continue doing that. Before coming to her house, he'd stopped by her shop. Elizabeth asked what he wanted, and her tone made it obvious she wasn't happy with him.

That was when he decided to let her know his feelings toward Cindi. As he talked, her manner grew less combative and more open. Finally, when he finished by saying he'd always pictured himself married to Cindi, she actually smiled.

"What is going on, Elizabeth?" he asked.

"There are some things you need to know." Elizabeth went on to explain how devastated Cindi was when he broke up with her. Then she told him how Cindi's parents' separation had affected her.

"I was surprised when Cindi told me they were separated. They always seemed like the perfect family," he said.

"There's no such thing as a perfect family. Her father was very busy with work, and her mother poured everything she had into her children. Once the children were gone, her mother felt lonely and suffered from a serious case of empty-nest syndrome. Unfortunately, her father still hasn't figured out he's got something to do with it. We're praying both of them will open their eyes and see the big picture."

"Wow," Jeremy said. "No wonder Cindi's become so disillusioned. I'm glad you told me. Why can't people be more open and honest with each other? That sure would solve a lot of problems."

She grinned. "Looks like you and Cindi have reached a point where you need to talk—and I mean *really* talk. You've been working so hard at being a businessman, and she's been busy trying to guard her heart."

As he thought about it, he realized she was right. "I guess it's time to rectify this situation."

"Just do yourself a favor and don't expect too much too fast, okay?" she said. "Now, do you need directions to her place?"

"Nope. I know exactly where she lives."

With a wide smile, she nodded. "I thought you might."

Now here he was sitting on her sofa, still immersed in silence. He was waiting for the right moment to propose.

"So what will you do now?" Cindi asked.

"I don't know," he said. "Before you ask me anything else, I have a question for you." *This is as good a time as any,* he figured as he mentally prepared himself to get down on one knee. He shifted slightly before she yanked on his hand.

"My answer is yes," she said, stunning him into silent immobility.

"Huh?"

"Yes, I'll sell my shop to you. I quit believing in the fairy tale, so it's no big deal to me anymore. And based on how you've gone to all this trouble, I think you'll do a good job with it, even if you do hire someone else to run it for you." She paused for a moment then added, "In fact, if you want me to, I can stick around and manage it until we get someone trained."

"Um, okay. . ." He wasn't sure what to say or do next. She'd just thwarted his first attempt at a marriage proposal. "I have another question for you," he said.

She leaned toward him. "What?"

"Did you really love me?"

All color drained from her face as she slowly nodded. "Yes, I did."

"How do you feel about me now?"

She quickly averted her gaze. "I don't know," she replied. Then she surprised him and looked him squarely in the eyes. "How about you? Did you really love me?"

"Yes," he replied, "very much. And I still do."

She blinked, turned red, then snickered. "You have an odd way of showing it, Jeremy."

"I made some mistakes when I was younger because I didn't have the slightest idea what to do. I've already told you I wanted to do the right thing and send you off to college without feeling like you had a ball and chain holding you back."

She shook her head. "Yes, you've said that, but like I told you, I never would have felt that way."

Tilting his head to one side, he studied her. There was something he wanted. . .no, needed to know. "If I hadn't been such a foolish kid and let you go, do you think we would have. . .well, you know."

Shaking her head, she said, "Would have what?"

"Do you think we might have ever gotten married?"

She looked stunned then quickly recovered. "I'm not sure.

I really meant it when I told you I loved you."

He felt a warmth travel from his heart to the rest of his body. But he couldn't dwell on what would have been. "Oh well, that's history. We need to move forward and try not to make the same mistakes."

"That's right," she agreed. "We have a whole future ahead of us, first with the sale of this business and then who knows what."

"Would you consider seeing where a relationship between us could go?" He cleared his throat and added, "I mean, if I do things right this time, will you consider. . .uh, going out with me and. . ."

She nodded. "Yes, Jeremy. I will. Just don't expect too much from me. I've been through a lot already, and I want to be cautious."

As he watched for any signs of remorse, he realized this was the happiest he'd seen her since he'd been back. Joy radiated from every pore.

"But nothing serious too fast," she added.

His insides fell, but he did his best to maintain his composure. "I'll take what I can get, just to be around you."

"So what do we do next?" she asked. "About the business, I mean."

He looked down so he could gather his thoughts and act like an intelligent businessman. "First of all, I need to get with Fran and sign the papers. There's the matter of negotiation, but I'll just pay your asking price, so that shouldn't be an issue. Since you said you'd run the shop until I know what I'm doing, I'll have an agreement drawn up."

"Sounds good." Her forehead crinkled for a split second, but she quickly recovered as she hopped up off the sofa and looked down at him. "I think we've just verbally agreed to a business deal."

As much as he wanted more from her than a business deal, that other stuff would have to wait. He wanted her to be a customer of her own shop, and he wanted her to stick around and run the place as long as they owned it, but that was something he'd tell her later. In the meantime, he'd have to settle for her willingness to sell him her shop, which was at least a move in the right direction.

fifteen

"Are you sure you want to go through with this?" Elizabeth asked the next morning after Cindi told her about her agreement with Jeremy.

"Positive." She felt a tiny tug at her heart, but she knew deep down this was the right thing. "But I'll still work here, and I'm sure he'll want you here, too."

"But when you leave, it won't be the same."

"Let's just take that as it comes," Cindi said. "I'm tired of worrying about things."

The next few days were busy with bridal appointments and real estate meetings with Fran. Cindi wanted things to go as smoothly as possible, and apparently, so did Jeremy. There was virtually no negotiation, with the exception of her agreement to run the shop. Cindi wanted a limited time on the agreement. Jeremy insisted on making it open-ended until he was sure he knew all the ins and outs of the business.

"I don't think he'll budge on this issue," Fran said. "But he can't keep you here against your will if you've shown you've acted in good faith."

Cindi finally agreed and signed the paperwork. The day after, she practically skipped into her shop. Elizabeth laughed. "You look like you've lost the weight of the world that's been sitting on your shoulders for months."

"That's exactly how I feel," Cindi replied.

"Oh, before I forget, your mother called right before you arrived. She wants you to call her back."

"I'll call later," Cindi said. "After—"

"She says it's urgent. Go call her now before our first appointment arrives."

"Okay," Cindi said as she lifted the phone and carried it to one of the fitting rooms.

She punched in her mother's number, and her dad answered. "Dad, what's going on? Is Mom there?"

"Yes, but I wanted to be the first to tell you we're getting back together. For good. I've moved back home."

"You have?" Cindi squealed. She forced herself to calm down. "That's wonderful news. What happened?"

"When your mother came by my office and told me what I did was inexcusable, I had no idea what she was talking about. I'd forgotten an appointment with the counselor, but I figured she could take care of that without me like she's always done before. Then I saw a side of your mother I'd never seen. She meant business this time." Cindi heard a little scuffling on the other side of the phone before her dad said, "Here, your mother wants to talk to you."

"Hey, Cindi, your father finally came to his senses."

"I'm super happy about this," Cindi said. "Want me to come over after work tonight?"

"Not tonight, sweetie. Your father's taking some time off from work, and we're heading out on a cruise first thing in the morning. He got us a good deal because some people canceled and they needed to fill that cabin."

"Let me know when you get back, okay?" Cindi said. "Tell Dad this is wonderful news, and y'all made my day."

"Will do. Love you, sweetie."

After she hung up, Cindi couldn't stop smiling. She walked out to the counter to put the phone back on the hook and caught Elizabeth staring at her.

"Why the silly grin?" Elizabeth asked.

"My mom and dad are back together, and it sounds like it

might stick this time."

Elizabeth jumped up and down, clapping like a little girl. "Way cool! That's the best news I've heard all day."

"It's only nine thirty in the morning," Cindi said, "and all is right in my world."

"I hope this sets the stage for a magnificent day." Elizabeth nodded toward the door. "Get ready for another round of excitement. Here comes the Pinkney-Armistead bridal party."

A few hours later, at noon, Jeremy walked in. "Wanna go for a walk in the park?"

Cindi snickered. "It's the middle of a workday."

Elizabeth nudged her. "Go ahead for a little while. We don't have another appointment until two. I can handle walk-ins."

"Why do I feel like I've been set up?" Cindi asked as she grabbed her purse from behind the counter.

Jeremy grinned at her. "Maybe because you have. I called Elizabeth and asked if you had any time available this week, and she said you weren't too busy today."

"That rascal. I'll have to talk to her."

To Cindi's surprise, Jeremy had a picnic basket packed. They went to a small park near the shop. "I didn't want to keep you away too long."

"This is really nice," Cindi said as she helped him spread the red-and-white-checkered cloth on the ground beneath an oak tree.

As they nibbled on sandwiches, Cindi felt herself relax. Jeremy talked about some of the houses he'd been looking at with Fran. "I'm just a little confused about what I'm looking for," he admitted.

"When you see the right house, you'll know it," Cindi said.

"Kind of like when a bride finds the right dress?" He looked her in the eye.

Slowly, she nodded. "Sort of like that, yes."

Jeremy put down his sandwich and reached for Cindi's hand. As he gently held it between both of his hands, he licked his lips then said, "You already know I've never stopped loving you, Cindi. And I just want to keep saying it over and over until you believe me."

Her heart hammered as she tried to think of a way to avoid admitting her feelings. But with him looking at her like that and the feelings washing through her, she knew she couldn't continue to run from him. Finally, she inhaled deeply, blinked, and smiled. "In spite of trying hard not to, I love you, too."

His smile brightened the day even more. Next thing she knew, she was in his arms, and his lips were softly on hers. "You couldn't have made me any happier than you just did," he whispered.

When they got back to the shop, Jeremy walked her to the door. "Thanks for the picnic," she said.

"It was all my pleasure," he replied. Cindi stood on the sidewalk and watched him walk to his car with a spring in his step before she turned around and went inside the shop.

"Well, you look like you've been up to something special," Elizabeth said. "What happened?"

Cindi briefly contemplated not saying anything and relishing her experience privately. But after all she'd been through with her best friend, she couldn't deny her the pleasure of this major turning point.

"Jeremy and I are in love," Cindi said with a sigh.

Elizabeth snickered. "I could've told you that. So what else is new?"

The next several days went by in a whirlwind of activity—both in the shop and after work. Jeremy was pulling out all the stops, not letting an opportunity go by without letting Cindi know how he felt. She loved every minute of it, too.

On the morning before they were supposed to transfer

ownership of the business, Cindi arrived early to look over the books one more time. Elizabeth was already there, putting some finishing touches on a gown she was personalizing for a bride. After their first appointment left, they went to the front of the showroom, where they heard commotion from outside.

Elizabeth frowned. "What's going on?"

A couple of men had set up some ladders and were now dropping some canvas on the sidewalk. "I have no idea. Let me go check." She went to the door and opened it just enough so they could hear her. "What's going on? What are y'all doing?"

"New owner just ordered a transitional sign until the new one he ordered can be made. He wanted us to come the day after tomorrow, but we had a cancellation today. We thought we'd go ahead and do it now." He stopped. "That is, if it's okay with you."

"I don't mind."

Cindi turned and told Elizabeth, who nodded. "Just tell them they need to move over when customers come in."

The guys said they were used to working around customers and they'd be happy to get out of the way. After she went back to the counter, Cindi didn't feel so carefree.

"What's the matter?" Elizabeth asked. "Seller's remorse?"

Cindi shrugged. "I have to admit I feel a little strange. I knew he was changing the name since I won't be the owner anymore. But this makes everything seem so final."

"Trust me, you'll be okay. It'll take some getting used to." She glanced over toward the men. "Do you think we should answer the phone with the new name?"

"Not until after the sale is final," Cindi said. "We're supposed to close on it tomorrow, but those guys weren't supposed to be here until the day after, so it's not really Jeremy's fault."

"Never said it was," Elizabeth said softly. "You're overthinking things again."

"Yeah, you're right. It's just that so much has happened lately, I'm not sure whether I'm coming or going."

"Do you regret selling this place?" Elizabeth asked. "I mean, now that your folks have gotten back together, maybe you see things differently."

Deep down, she did sort of regret it, but it was too late now. "I can't allow myself to regret anything," Cindi admitted. "I just need to focus on what's ahead."

"Good attitude."

They had a couple of morning appointments. Then they had several walk-ins that afternoon, but they didn't have another set appointment until late afternoon. The guys hanging the sign finished midafternoon. Finally, after the last appointment left, Elizabeth gathered her belongings to leave. Her eyes darted, and she seemed a little nervous as she moved toward the door.

"Are you okay?" Cindi asked.

"Uh, sure, I'm fine. Just eager to get out of here."

"What's going on?" Cindi stared hard at her friend, who'd finally made it to the door.

"Nothing. See you in the morning," she said as she carefully opened the door and quickly stepped onto the sidewalk.

Cindi watched her friend walk toward her car then turn around. Suddenly Elizabeth's eyebrows shot up, and she started laughing as she pointed to the sign. She spotted Cindi and motioned for her to come outside.

Her behavior is bizarre, Cindi thought as she went to see what Elizabeth was pointing to. When she turned around, she saw the sign. There in big, bold letters was a sign above the door that read CINDI AND JEREMY'S BRIDAL BOUTIQUE.

"Wha—?" She looked at Elizabeth, who was still laughing.

"Don't ask me," Elizabeth finally said when she calmed down. "Ask him." She pointed to the door where Jeremy stood.

Cindi glared at Elizabeth. "I'll discuss this with you later." Then she marched right up to the shop and went inside. "What is going on?" she demanded. "Why does the sign say. . . CINDI AND JEREMY'S BOUTIQUE?"

"Correction," he said. "It's CINDI AND JEREMY'S *BRIDAL* BOUTIQUE."

"Okay, whatever. Why does it say that?"

He shrugged. "It's the transitional sign until—"

"I know. The workers already told me, 'until the permanent sign is made.' But what's going on with this?" She went outside again and looked at it, then walked back in.

"I figured since you were staying on for a while and—"

"How did you get in here? I didn't see you walk in."

Jeremy hung his head. "Elizabeth let me in the back door. Don't be upset with her. I talked her into it."

"What is going on, Jeremy? I—"

He closed the gap between them and got down on one knee, which silenced her. When he pulled out a little black box and opened it, her breath caught in her throat.

"Well?" he asked. "Will you marry me?"

Cindi started to sway as she felt light-headed. Then she caught sight of the bridal gown behind him—the one she'd tried on and loved. "Stay right where you are," she ordered. "And whatever you do, don't turn around."

"Huh?" He started to turn.

She reached down, turned his face toward her, and repeated, "Don't turn around. I'll be right back."

"Um. . .okay."

She quickly ran toward the dress, grabbed it off the hook, and carried it into the stock room. When she came back out, she got into position in front of Jeremy. "Now where were we?"

"What was that all about?" he asked.

"I had to hide the dress. You're not supposed to see it until the wedding day when I walk down the aisle."

A wide grin spread across his face. "Oh, okay."

"That doesn't let you off the hook, though," she said. "Back to what you were saying."

Still smiling, he took her hand, kissed the back of it, and said, "Cindi Clark, will you make me the happiest man in the world and be my wife?"

"Of course I will!"

epilogue

"I still can't get over how perfect this dress is," Elizabeth said. "You could have tried wedding gowns on all day and not found one that looked as good as this one."

Cindi looked at her reflection in the three-way mirror and nodded. "I know. It's like a fairy tale. Sort of a twist on Cinderella."

Elizabeth went to the other mirror and refreshed her makeup, leaving Cindi alone. Her parents stood off to the side having their own private moment, which was a wonder in itself.

The usher came and got her mother. Cindi could tell her dad was nervous by the way he played with his tie. This was a day she'd never forget—one of miracles and a joy she never dreamed she'd realize.

When the music changed, Elizabeth jumped. "There's my cue. See ya at the altar." She got to the door, paused, and said, "After all this, I hope you never doubt Jeremy's love for you."

"Trust me, I won't," Cindi replied.

Elizabeth gave their familiar thumbs-up gesture; then she was off and marching down the aisle. Cindi couldn't help but laugh, because this was a one-eighty for Elizabeth, who'd been the most protective person of all.

Cindi's dad turned to her and extended his arm. "Ready, sweetheart?"

She nodded and took his arm. As she took her first steps, she sent up a prayer of thanks to the Lord for softening her heart and bringing her true love back. Then she locked gazes with Jeremy, whose smile warmed her heart and reassured her that she was about to embark on the journey of a lifetime— with the Lord's blessing.

A Letter To Our Readers

Dear Reader:

In order that we might better contribute to your reading enjoyment, we would appreciate your taking a few minutes to respond to the following questions. We welcome your comments and read each form and letter we receive. When completed, please return to the following:

Fiction Editor
Heartsong Presents
PO Box 719
Uhrichsville, Ohio 44683

1. Did you enjoy reading *If the Dress Fits* by Debby Mayne?
   ❏ Very much! I would like to see more books by this author!
   ❏ Moderately. I would have enjoyed it more if

   _____

   _____

   _____

2. Are you a member of **Heartsong Presents**? ❏ Yes ❏ No
   If no, where did you purchase this book? _____

   _____

3. How would you rate, on a scale from 1 (poor) to 5 (superior),
   the cover design? _____

4. On a scale from 1 (poor) to 10 (superior), please rate the
   following elements.

   ____ Heroine   ____ Plot
   ____ Hero   ____ Inspirational theme
   ____ Setting   ____ Secondary characters

5. These characters were special because? _____

_____

_____

6. How has this book inspired your life? _____

_____

_____

7. What settings would you like to see covered in future
   Heartsong Presents books? _____

_____

_____

8. What are some inspirational themes you would like to see
   treated in future books? _____

_____

_____

9. Would you be interested in reading other **Heartsong
   Presents** titles? ❑ Yes   ❑ No

10. Please check your age range:
    ❑ Under 18   ❑ 18-24
    ❑ 25-34   ❑ 35-45
    ❑ 46-55   ❑ Over 55

Name _____

Occupation _____

Address _____

City, State, Zip_____

OHIO
Weddings

3 stories in 1

Step onto Bay Island and be touched by love. In a small Ohio community on Lake Erie, three remarkable women reexamine their lives. Will these three women ever be the same after the waves of change set their hearts adrift?

Contemporary, paperback, 368 pages, 5³⁄₁₆" x 8"

Please send me _____ copies of *Ohio Weddings*. I am enclosing $6.97 for each. (Please add $3.00 to cover postage and handling per order. OH add 7% tax. If outside the U.S. please call 740-922-7280 for shipping charges.)

Name_____

Address _____

City, State, Zip _____

To place a credit card order, call 1-740-922-7280.
Send to: Heartsong Presents Readers' Service, PO Box 721, Uhrichsville, OH 44683

Hearts♥ng

Any 12
Heartsong
Presents titles
for only
$27.00*

CONTEMPORARY ROMANCE IS CHEAPER BY THE DOZEN!

Buy any assortment of twelve *Heartsong Presents* titles and save 25% off the already discounted price of $2.97 each!

*plus $3.00 shipping and handling per order and sales tax where applicable. If outside the U.S. please call 740-922-7280 for shipping charges.

HEARTSONG PRESENTS TITLES AVAILABLE NOW:

___HP517 *The Neighborly Thing to Do,* W. E. Brunstetter
___HP518 *For a Father's Love,* J. A. Grote
___HP521 *Be My Valentine,* J. Livingston
___HP522 *Angel's Roost,* J. Spaeth
___HP525 *Game of Pretend,* J. Odell
___HP526 *In Search of Love,* C. Lynxwiler
___HP529 *Major League Dad,* K. Y'Barbo
___HP530 *Joe's Diner,* G. Sattler
___HP533 *On a Clear Day,* Y. Lehman
___HP534 *Term of Love,* M. Pittman Crane
___HP537 *Close Enough to Perfect,* T. Fowler
___HP538 *A Storybook Finish,* L. Bliss
___HP541 *The Summer Girl,* A. Boeshaar
___HP545 *Love Is Patient,* C. M. Hake
___HP546 *Love Is Kind,* J. Livingston
___HP549 *Patchwork and Politics,* C. Lynxwiler
___HP550 *Woodhaven Acres,* B. Etchison
___HP553 *Bay Island,* B. Loughner
___HP554 *A Donut a Day,* G. Sattler
___HP557 *If You Please,* T. Davis
___HP558 *A Fairy Tale Romance,* M. Panagiotopoulos
___HP561 *Ton's Vow,* K. Cornelius
___HP562 *Family Ties,* J. L. Barton
___HP565 *An Unbreakable Hope,* K. Billerbeck
___HP566 *The Baby Quilt,* J. Livingston
___HP569 *Ageless Love,* L. Bliss
___HP570 *Beguiling Masquerade,* C. G. Page
___HP573 *In a Land Far Far Away,* M. Panagiotopoulos
___HP574 *Lambert's Pride,* L. A. Coleman and R. Hauck
___HP577 *Anita's Fortune,* K. Cornelius
___HP578 *The Birthday Wish,* J. Livingston
___HP581 *Love Online,* K. Billerbeck
___HP582 *The Long Ride Home,* A. Boeshaar
___HP585 *Compassion's Charm,* D. Mills

___HP586 *A Single Rose,* P. Griffin
___HP589 *Changing Seasons,* C. Reece and J. Reece-Demarco
___HP590 *Secret Admirer,* G. Sattler
___HP593 *Angel Incognito,* J. Thompson
___HP594 *Out on a Limb,* G. Gaymer Martin
___HP597 *Let My Heart Go,* B. Huston
___HP598 *More Than Friends,* T. H. Murray
___HP601 *Timing is Everything,* T. V. Bateman
___HP602 *Dandelion Bride,* J. Livingston
___HP605 *Picture Imperfect,* N. J. Farrier
___HP606 *Mary's Choice,* Kay Cornelius
___HP609 *Through the Fire,* C. Lynxwiler
___HP613 *Chorus of One,* J. Thompson
___HP614 *Forever in My Heart,* L. Ford
___HP617 *Run Fast, My Love,* P. Griffin
___HP618 *One Last Christmas,* J. Livingston
___HP621 *Forever Friends,* T. H. Murray
___HP622 *Time Will Tell,* L. Bliss
___HP625 *Love's Image,* D. Mayne
___HP626 *Down From the Cross,* J. Livingston
___HP629 *Look to the Heart,* T. Fowler
___HP630 *The Flat Marriage Fix,* K. Hayse
___HP633 *Longing for Home,* C. Lynxwiler
___HP634 *The Child Is Mine,* M. Colvin
___HP637 *Mother's Day,* J. Livingston
___HP638 *Real Treasure,* T. Davis
___HP641 *The Pastor's Assignment,* K. O'Brien
___HP642 *What's Cooking,* G. Sattler
___HP645 *The Hunt for Home,* G. Aiken
___HP649 *4th of July,* J. Livingston
___HP650 *Romanian Rhapsody,* D. Franklin
___HP653 *Lakeside,* M. Davis
___HP654 *Alaska Summer,* M. H. Flinkman
___HP657 *Love Worth Finding,* C. M. Hake
___HP658 *Love Worth Keeping,* J. Livingston
___HP661 *Lambert's Code,* R. Hauck
___HP665 *Bah Humbug, Mrs. Scrooge,* J. Livingston

(If ordering from this page, please remember to include it with the order form.)

Presents

__HP666	*Sweet Charity*, J. Thompson	__HP729	*Bay Hideaway*, B. Loughner
__HP669	*The Island*, M. Davis	__HP730	*With Open Arms*, J. L. Barton
__HP670	*Miss Menace*, N. Lavo	__HP733	*Safe in His Arms*, T. Davis
__HP673	*Flash Flood*, D. Mills	__HP734	*Larkspur Dreams*, A. Higman and
__HP677	*Banking on Love*, J. Thompson		J. A. Thompson
__HP678	*Lambert's Peace*, R. Hauck	__HP737	*Darcy's Inheritance*, L. Ford
__HP681	*The Wish*, L. Bliss	__HP738	*Picket Fence Pursuit*, J. Johnson
__HP682	*The Grand Hotel*, M. Davis	__HP741	*The Heart of the Matter*, K. Dykes
__HP685	*Thunder Bay*, B. Loughner	__HP742	*Prescription for Love*, A. Boeshaar
__HP686	*Always a Bridesmaid*, A. Boeshaar	__HP745	*Family Reunion*, J. L. Barton
__HP689	*Unforgettable*, J. L. Barton	__HP746	*By Love Acquitted*, Y. Lehman
__HP690	*Heritage*, M. Davis	__HP749	*Love by the Yard*, G. Sattler
__HP693	*Dear John*, K. V. Sawyer	__HP750	*Except for Grace*, T. Fowler
__HP694	*Riches of the Heart*, T. Davis	__HP753	*Long Trail to Love*, P. Griffin
__HP697	*Dear Granny*, P. Griffin	__HP754	*Red Like Crimson*, J. Thompson
__HP698	*With a Mother's Heart*, J. Livingston	__HP757	*Everlasting Love*, L. Ford
__HP701	*Cry of My Heart*, L. Ford	__HP758	*Wedded Bliss*, K. Y'Barbo
__HP702	*Never Say Never*, L. N. Dooley	__HP761	*Double Blessing*, D. Mayne
__HP705	*Listening to Her Heart*, J. Livingston	__HP762	*Photo Op*, L. A. Coleman
__HP706	*The Dwelling Place*, K. Miller	__HP765	*Sweet Sugared Love*, P. Griffin
__HP709	*That Wilder Boy*, K. V. Sawyer	__HP766	*Pursuing the Goal*, J. Johnson
__HP710	*To Love Again*, J. L. Barton	__HP769	*Who Am I?*, L. N. Dooley
__HP713	*Secondhand Heart*, J. Livingston	__HP770	*And Baby Makes Five*, G. G. Martin
__HP714	*Anna's Journey*, N. Toback	__HP773	*A Matter of Trust*, L. Harris
__HP717	*Merely Players*, K. Kovach	__HP774	*The Groom Wore Spurs*, J. Livingston
__HP718	*In His Will*, C. Hake	__HP777	*Seasons of Love*, E. Goddard
__HP721	*Through His Grace*, K. Hake	__HP778	*The Love Song*, J. Thompson
__HP722	*Christmas Mommy*, T. Fowler	__HP781	*Always Yesterday*, J. Odell
__HP725	*By His Hand*, J. Johnson	__HP782	*Trespassed Hearts*, L. A. Coleman
__HP726	*Promising Angela*, K. V. Sawyer		

Great Inspirational Romance at a Great Price!

Heartsong Presents books are inspirational romances in
contemporary and historical settings, designed to give you an
enjoyable, spirit-lifting reading experience. You can choose
wonderfully written titles from some of today's best authors like
Wanda E. Brunstetter, Mary Connealy, Susan Page Davis,
Cathy Marie Hake, Joyce Livingston, and many others.

When ordering quantities less than twelve, above titles are $2.97 each.
Not all titles may be available at time of order.

SEND TO: **Heartsong Presents** Readers' Service
P.O. Box 721, Uhrichsville, Ohio 44683

Please send me the items checked above. I am enclosing $ _____
(please add $3.00 to cover postage per order. OH add 7% tax. WA
add 8.5%). Send check or money order, no cash or C.O.D.s, please.

To place a credit card order, call 1-740-922-7280.

NAME _____

ADDRESS _____

CITY/STATE _____ ZIP_____

HP 3-08

HEARTSONG
PRESENTS

If you love Christian romance...

$10.⁹⁹

You'll love Heartsong Presents' inspiring and faith-filled romances by today's very best Christian authors...Wanda E. Brunstetter, Mary Connealy, Susan Page Davis, Cathy Marie Hake, and Joyce Livingston, to mention a few!

When you join Heartsong Presents, you'll enjoy four brand-new, mass market, 176-page books—two contemporary and two historical—that will build you up in your faith when you discover God's role in every relationship you read about!

Mass Market 176 Pages

Imagine...four new romances every four weeks—with men and women like you who long to meet the one God has chosen as the love of their lives...all for the low price of $10.99 postpaid.

To join, simply visit www.heartsong presents.com or complete the coupon below and mail it to the address provided.

YES! Sign me up for Heartsong!

NEW MEMBERSHIPS WILL BE SHIPPED IMMEDIATELY!
Send no money now. We'll bill you only $10.99 postpaid with your first shipment of four books. Or for faster action, call 1-740-922-7280.

NAME _____

ADDRESS_____

CITY_____ STATE _____ ZIP _____

MAIL TO: HEARTSONG PRESENTS, P.O. Box 721, Uhrichsville, Ohio 44683
or sign up at WWW.HEARTSONGPRESENTS.COM